CATRINAS

Garry Ryan

A Detectives Jackson and Lane Mystery

Pages Press

P
• • •
Pages Press...
Books on Kensington
1135 Kensington Rd. NW, Calgary, AB Canada T2N 3P4
www.pageskensington.com

Typeset in Minion

Editors: Kendra Gaede, Jeremy Shannon
Cover art: Laura Barrett
Interior design: Kendra Gaede
Author Photo: Ella Towers

LIBRARY AND ARCHIVES CANADA CATALOGUING IN PUBLICATION

Title: Catrinas / Garry Ryan
Names: Ryan, Garry 1953– author.

Issued in print and electronic formats.
ISBN 978-1-9995135-2-8 (softcover)
ISBN 978-1-9995135-3-5 (e-book)

For Sharon,
Karma, Ben,
Luke, Indy, Ella
and Parisa

CHAPTER 1

Lauren Jackson started the engine of her Tacoma pickup, powered down the window, inhaling the scent from lilacs, thick with their May mauve perfume.

Jackson reached into the side pocket of her black and white yoga bag, sliding her phone out. She loosed her shoulder-length brunette hair, combing it back with her fingers, taking an elastic from her teeth to tie it into a ponytail, enjoying the cooler air flowing from the vents.

Her green eyes narrowed when the phone rang; thumb pressing the button on the steering wheel to answer, "Jackson."

"It's Nigel. We've got a situation."

Lauren pulled her seatbelt over, snapping it into the lock. "Where?"

"I'm texting you the address now."

"What kind of situation?"

"Apparent homicide. You're the lead on this one. Just do what you do."

It took fifteen minutes to cross the river, head up Bow Trail and pull up out front of a 1,000 square foot bungalow in Glendale. Her uncle liked to tell her how he'd bought a house like this in the 1950s for $11,000. They now sold for half a million.

She parked across the street, taking in the scene. The blue and white forensics van was parked within the yellow crime scene tape wrapped around mature tree trunks and a light pole. Another black and white van was parked outside the tape. An ambulance sat nearby with its back door open.

A man sat on the floor, his eyes wide with shock, wearing an oxygen mask, grey blanket, sweats and T-shirt. She estimated he was just under six feet and just over 200 pounds. Lauren turned, taking in the house with its new windows and doors, a bow window and grey stucco. She noted some of the shingles curling on the roof.

That seems out of place, Lauren thought.

One of the forensic team stepped out the front door wearing the requisite white bunny suit and full-face respirator.

Jackson climbed out of her truck, walking across the street, nodding at the uniformed officer near the black and white SUV. She ducked under the tape, stopping in front of the man taking off his respirator. She recognized Sindhu, who had two strips of sweaty black hair stuck to either side of his head.

"When can I take a look?" she asked.

Sindhu looked at her pink running shoes, black clam diggers and neon orange tank top. "Now if you like. You'll need one of these." He held up the respirator, "There's an extra mask in there," pointing at the forensics van, nodding at the ambulance parked down the street. "Bear spray." Sindhu walked to the back of the van, lifting out a mask, handing it to her. "It's still pretty intense inside."

"Thanks." She took the mask, pulling it on, adjusting the straps, walking up the sidewalk and through the front door.

The hallway led straight to the bathroom where a body lay on its left side, head pointing into the kitchen, torso blocking the hallway and feet across the bathroom entrance.

As she moved closer, she saw the white porcelain lid from the toilet tank on the floor. The right side of the man's skull was indented. He wore blue latex gloves. Near the right fingertips, a black handgun with a silencer adorned with the red emblem of a phoenix on the grip. She recognized the Ruger .22 calibre while pulling out her cellphone, using it to take a photo of the serial number. Beyond the Ruger, an orange can of bear spray lay on the beige tile of the bathroom floor. She photographed the white label on the bottom of the bear spray. She crouched, seeing a round hole in the white tile wall just under the opaque window.

"Jackson?"

Lauren turned without standing, seeing a uniformed officer on the front step. "What's up?" Her voice was muffled, the visor beginning to fog.

"The ambulance is ready to leave."

She stood, pointing at the open front door. "Not yet!"

Paul Lane sat next to a window overlooking Kensington Road, the pedestrian and vehicle traffic and the white and blue Plaza Theatre. Pages Books had people out front perusing used books. Next to that was a black shop with white letters – TRAPPED.

Paul checked for messages on his cell phone with his right hand, lifting and draining a mochaccino with his left. His hair was entirely white and cut short. The scar on his earlobe was emphasized by a sunken cheek.

He looked up when Scott set another cup in front of him. He smiled at the short-haired, rough-shaven Hexagon barista in the striped shirt. "Thanks. You read my mind."

He smiled. "You usually have at least two."

Lane stood up, taking the lid from the empty cup, pressing it onto the new. "Time to go and pick up the kids." He set three toonies on the counter.

Scott took the empty cup. "See you tomorrow?"

"Always."

Lane walked out the open front door, stepping down the

curved stairway, turning right onto the sidewalk paralleling Kensington Road, walking west toward 14th Street. He passed a vintage clothing store, then a sub shop and a drug store before stopping at the lights.

An unmuffled motorcycle engine echoed off the buildings. Paul turned to see a man riding a yellow Harley. He wore black leather, a German-style helmet and skeleton face bandana.

Arthur would have said something about macho boys attracting mates by putting something powerful between their thighs. Lane waited for the walk signal before continuing West.

Jackson stood at the back of the ambulance where an EMT with short blonde hair, wore navy blue and a stethoscope. The wide-eyed, white-faced patient was eye to eye with Jackson, perched on the floor of the ambulance. His black hair stuck up at odd, uncombed angles and he breathed through an oxygen mask. He had the telltale fifty-metre stare of someone who's been shit scared.

"Is he stable?"

The EMT's name tag – 'Shirley' – became visible as she turned. "He is."

Jackson said, "I'd like him fingerprinted."

Shirley's eyebrows created a crease across her forehead.

"For his own protection."

The eyebrows dropped.

Jackson put a hand on Sindhu's shoulder while facing the patient. "My friend is very good at his job. It will only take a moment, then a police escort will be accompanying you to the hospital."

She turned, half expecting some kind of argument, ready with a reply. When none came, she went back to the house, putting on the respirator. She began a systematic search of the bedrooms, living room and kitchen before going downstairs.

The basement walls were finished in knotty pine, a blue carpet on the floor, cooler air collecting there. An elliptical and some hand weights were arranged on this side of a doorway cutting the basement in half.

In one corner, a green plastic bin spilled over with spent energy drinks. She walked to the open door, stepping into a room with a widescreen TV attached to the south wall. Beneath the wide screen were three computer monitors, two keyboards and three CPUs. She took in the room and what it might or might not imply before pulling out her cell phone, taking a series of pictures.

After ten minutes, she heard soft soles descending the stairs. She turned to see Sindhu without a respirator.

"The calendar boys brought some fans, opened the windows and cleared out the worst of the bear spray."

Lauren pulled off her mask, setting it on the black office chair. She pushed her fingers back through her hair. "Fingerprints?"

"None of Dave's on the Ruger. His prints match the ones on the porcelain lid and the bear spray. Those are initial findings. I'll check them again when I get to the lab but it appears to be pretty clear-cut." He looked at the computers. "This guy a hacker?"

"Dave got a last name?"

"Singer."

She looked at a chart on the wall to the right of one of the monitors. The acronyms WTF and CNIG were hand-written, circled and situated in the centre of a web of lines and circles. "Any ID on the body?"

Sindhu held up a plastic evidence bag. Inside, a pair of black keyless remote fobs were connected with a cable. "Just the keys to a rental. And, I checked – no prints."

"Mind if we take a quick drive around the neighbourhood?"

Five minutes later, they found a grey Chrysler whose lights flashed when Sindhu pressed the fob. It only took a few minutes to circle the vehicle with yellow crime scene tape.

Lane walked west along 2nd Avenue, taking opportunities to inhale a variety of fragrances from the blossoms encountered on the way.

Arthur always loved this time of year and the scent of the lilacs. He would stop in the middle of a conversation to inhale the blossoms.

Lane looked ahead to the south end of Queen Mary School where Ella went to kindergarten and Indy was in grade two. It was a collection of newer square edges and older more gothic lines just across the river from the centre of downtown.

He crossed the street, stepping on the grass. He passed through a gate, looking past the playground to the side door where parents gathered.

He felt the grass brushing his ankles, looked up at the forty metre tops of the trees, then back to the school. The double doors opened, freeing children in sunglasses, shorts, T-shirts, flashing running shoes and backpacks half the height of the five-year-olds.

Ella was first out, her blonde hair tied back, wearing a blue T-shirt and pink shorts, searching the sea of adult faces. She spotted Lane, walking over to stand next, handing him her backpack. He retrieved a granola bar from the stash in his pants pocket. He used his teeth to open the wrapper, handing it to her.

Ella took the bar, looking up at him. "Can we play?"

He looked at his watch. "Ten minutes?"

She ran to the playground.

Indy was out a minute later: taller, brown hair, grey T-shirt, black shorts, repeating the process of handing Lane his backpack, accepting the food and running to join a game of soccer.

Lane stood under the shade of a tree, adopting the familiar protective posture, turning one way, then the other, keeping both children in view. He glanced at the road where a mother and father helped their son into the backseat of a black SUV towing a trailer more than twice its size. A flashback to a car and trailer on its back, flipped by a 90-kilometre wind gust. The parents in the front seat crushed, their screaming child in the backseat. Lane first on the scene in his blues, releasing the child, tears and snot running down her face.

Brenda Bruciarsi was the only woman at the conference table. It was her comfort zone. At five-foot-one, 150 pounds, she was the shortest in the room and a match for any mind or mouth.

She'd been offered a position at Wright Trust Financial after working for the PMO for a decade where she'd earned a reputation as the most powerful woman in Ottawa. WTF came to her about halfway through her tenure with the PMO, tentatively at first, then more aggressively when it became obvious Prime Minister Ross Reed's mandate was done.

Freddy Wright, the 70-year-old developer and golfer with dyed black hair, came to her without any preamble. "We need you at WTF. You've got the connections and we need to know the best ways to manage risks to our assets."

She'd moved to Calgary six months ago to find herself in the middle of this shit storm, surrounded by men who slicked their hair back, members of the same golf club, the same church, the same political party and board members of WTF.

They turned to her as she entered the room, taking her assigned seat at the massive solid oak table. She pulled her smart phone from the right pocket of her red leather jacket, then the burner from her left, setting them on the table either side of a teacup.

Brenda brushed a millimetre of white fluff from the thigh

of her black slacks, reminding herself about her role here. It was the same one she'd had at the PMO: fix it, solve it, keep the boss's hands clean. Save their money and reputations. Money came first, always – reputations, a photo finish second.

Wright's voice was crushed gravel when he said, "Give us the update Brenda."

She held up the burner phone. "No contact with our guy. Nothing to report as yet."

"Our guy?" Colin Wright had more grey hair in stark contrast to his father, chairman Wright.

Senior Wright held up his hands, palms out, stopping talk or traffic – it was difficult to tell which.

Brenda remembered her research on junior Wright. He'd had his feet burned at a motivational speaker's event in the U.S. Colin required skin grafts after attempting to find his personal power by walking over a bed of coals. *He and his father are so confident, yet so open to suggestion as long as it's what they want to hear.* "The situation in Mexico City is contained."

Colin turned his back to his father, then asked, "Are we still being blackmailed or not?"

"Too soon to tell." Brenda took the phones off the table, tucking them in her pockets, standing. "Excuse me while I gather more information on the situation." She nodded at the senior Wright. "You will be updated when more facts become available."

She walked to the door, opening it, heading outside.

The office was situated in a strip mall with brick walls and red-tiled roofs. She climbed into her grey Ford SUV parked out front of the WTF office, pulling out her phone, plugging it in, opening the audio recording and emailing it home.

Brenda understood how important it was for a fall girl to have insurance.

YYC TV NEWS LIVE

"Hello, and welcome to YYC News Live. I'm Stephanie Ozduran. Calgary Police are currently investigating a suspicious death reported in the city's southwest. We go live now to YYC's Natasha Summerville, who is on the scene."

A reporter stands in front of a blue and white forensic van, parked by a bungalow surrounded by yellow crime scene tape. She wears glasses, a red scarf, blue jacket and jeans, tucking a wayward strand of red hair behind her left ear while listening to her earpiece.

"Thank you, Stephanie. As you can see behind me, Calgary police are investigating the discovery today of a man's body in this southwest home. The police have yet to reveal details about the victim. Another man, thought to be the homeowner, was also found on scene and is now in hospital. Early indications are this is a homicide – the fourteenth in the city so far. Natasha Summerville, YYC News, Calgary."

"Thank you, Natasha. Stay tuned to YYC News. We will continue to provide updates about this suspicious death as more details become available."

Lane stood at Christine and Dan's kitchen sink, watching the kids through the window to the backyard. It was lined on three sides by a chain link fence, its wire interwoven with honeysuckle hinting at blooms, lilacs in delicious purple and Colorado blue spruce trees at the corners.

Ella watched Indy kick his soccer ball at the red-framed net in the middle of the yard. Then she began riding her coaster bike in circles on the patio.

Lane looked down, slicing a red pepper in half. His fingers

held the cooler flesh on the inside as the knife cut slivers. He stopped, looking out the window as Indy watched his sister, calculating distance and speed as she circled.

Lane tapped the window with the knife handle. Indy turned away from his sister, kicking the ball into the net instead.

Lauren walked into the square, white stucco building in northeast Calgary. A fire hall was attached to the north side. Four calendar boys were washing a pumper. Two checked over their shoulders to see if she noticed.

Inside, she spotted Rhonda, the ever-present force of nature who kept the homicide detectives in line. She was thirty, brown-haired and eyed, five-foot-four and mother of two.

Lauren remembered a very bad day about six months ago. A missing toddler's body had been found after three days of non-stop police work. They'd all been sleeping on the floor, eating on the run, tracking down leads. Hashir Wajdan was also thirty, father of three, black-haired, six-foot-three, with a booming voice.

The next day he'd lost a file, standing over Rhonda's desk, demanding she find it. Rhonda tearfully called him an asshole. Thirty minutes later the file was found under a pile on Hashir's desk. After that, he endured every shit detail on their shift: going door-to-door, tracking credit card and phone bills. It lasted thirty days, until Rhonda called an end to it. Hashir evolved into Rhonda's fiercest protector.

When a much touted, hyphenated, newly arrived member from the UK got handsy with Rhonda, Nigel warned him. When the new member ignored the warning and grabbed Rhonda's ass, Hashir went nose-to-nose before Nigel had a chance. The hyphenated detective was gone that afternoon.

Lauren smiled and asked, "What's up?"

Rhonda had her phone tucked between her shoulder and

right ear. "I'm on hold. Nigel's asking for you."

Lauren went to the door of Nigel's office, knocking once. It opened. Nigel's face appeared. His black hair was cut short, framing a round, freckled face on a lean frame. He waved her in, then spoke into his phone. "Gotta go." He pressed 'end', moving around behind his desk, balancing on his feet like a boxer before sitting.

She sat down in front of him. "What's up?"

"You've got an officer guarding this..." He picked up his phone, thumbing through his texts. "... David Singer?"

Lauren nodded. "The scene has the earmarks of a professional hit. The gunman wore rubber gloves. The gun's a silenced Ruger .22." She paused, knowing he would understand a silenced .22 meant no fuss and likely no messy exit wound from a headshot.

"Any idea why a contractor would want to kill Singer?"

"All we have right now is a shocked, scared Singer and a basement filled with sophisticated computer equipment."

"How did Singer manage to take the contractor down?"

"Bear spray, then hit him up against the side of the head with a porcelain toilet tank lid."

Nigel looked past her to the door. "Was Singer expecting trouble?'

Lauren nodded. "That's my guess, why else have bear spray when you go to the can?"

"When do you interview Singer?"

She looked at her wristwatch. "I was thinking in an hour from now; let the adrenalin and the shock wear off."

"Okay if I come along?"

"Because?"

"Interest. Never dealt with a contract hit. And my wife is a computer genius. I might have some insights."

Lauren looked over her shoulder at her desk. "Let me check a few details first."

Christine opened the front door, dropping bags, kicking off shoes, crouching to Ella's height, engulfing her in a hug. Indy waited, hoping to be noticed, standing at his mother's shoulder. All of this took place in an aromatic cloud of fried red peppers with overtones of sizzling maple breakfast sausages.

Christine smiled up at Lane, her eyes bright. In that moment Lane flashed back to their first meeting: Christine was hours old with her dark hair, him feeling fierce, protective love.

He almost smiled.

"Supper smells great! Thanks." She squeezed her babes 'til they complained then said, "Wash your hands so we can eat!"

After the wash up, Lane followed the clan into the kitchen where Ella hoarded sausages, Indy laughed at the farting ketchup bottle, the fried red peppers were a surprising hit, and the dessert popsicles an even bigger one. The kids headed outside to slurp them in the backyard.

Christine stood at the kitchen window watching the kids, teaming up with Lane to stack dishes in the dishwasher before turning to say, "Thanks for helping with the kids. I don't know what I'd do without you."

Lane looked at the front door and his shoes, sensing the conversation was about to take them down a more serious path.

Christine wiped her hands on a tea towel, leaning against the counter to see her kids out the right eye and her uncle out the left. She was close to six feet tall, with cinnamon skin, black hair trimmed shoulder length, wearing a yellow blouse and black slacks. "Summer's coming. Are you thinking about a holiday?"

Lane set his feet shoulder length apart. From where he stood, he could cover the kids in the yard. "Hadn't thought about it."

"Lola wants us to visit them in La Jola."

Lane cringed at the mention of Lola, Dan's mother, entrepreneur of the year, force of nature, multi-millionaire, angel of darkness and the person (it was rumoured) who could bullshit better than Trump. "What's Dan think?"

"He's got a one week break from the movie. Says it's up to me."

"The kids would have fun at the beach." He felt something like dread rising up from south of the scar on his abdomen.

"I was talking to Alex, Matt and Linda. We have a different plan we'd like to run past you."

He saw Ella's popsicle fall from the stick. He walked over to the fridge, grabbing two more treats, heading for the back door. Ella was looking at the stick, then looking back to the red melting mass on the patio. Her lower lip was beginning to quiver as he blew open the plastic packaging of the new treat, handing it to her.

Indy said, "Hey!"

Lane held up the second treat. Indy nodded, his argument about fairness irrelevant.

Christine stood next to Lane, eyeing Ella, who said, "Thank you."

Lane blew the second wrapping open, handing the red treat to Indy who looked at his Mom and said, "Thank you."

Christine put her hand on Lane's shoulder. "We'd like you to come with us. We were thinking of a place in Kelowna. It's close to the beach. Linda is making the arrangements. We've had a rough year and we thought it would be nice to get together in happier circumstances."

Lane tried to choke out a reply. Instead he wiped the back of his hand across his eyes, feeling Christine's arm around his shoulders, the warmth of her embrace.

Dave Singer sat in a vinyl chair the colour of vomit. He faced the window. The glass gave a view of the doors to the ambulance garage. The cinder block walls of the room were painted such a pale version of urine, even Lauren's indifferent sensibilities were offended.

Singer still wore his sweats and T-shirt. He looked over his shoulder when Lauren opened the door to the meeting room just down the hall from the nursing station. They were in the emergency wing of the Foothills Medical Centre.

Lauren said, "You look better."

Dave nodded, looking at the red folder in her right hand. Then he looked at Nigel as he closed the door. "Who's he?"

"Nigel Li, Detective with Calgary Police Service." Nigel pulled the ID from his jacket pocket, handing it to Dave who was in the process of dragging his chair around to face the detectives.

Lauren pulled a chair to within a metre of his before sitting down. Nigel did the same. She lifted the cell phone from the pocket of her navy blazer, setting it on an end table, turning it on. "This conversation is being recorded. Do you want a lawyer present?"

"No." Dave grabbed the left-hand short sleeve of his T-shirt with his right-hand, stretching the fabric, twisting his head, wiping the sweat along his hairline "The guy had a gun. He was going to kill me. I had no choice!"

Lauren crossed her right leg over the left. "Walk us through it. When did you know there was someone else in the house?"

Dave looked at Nigel. "I was on the shitter and I heard the hallway floorboards creaking."

Nigel raised an eyebrow.

Dave said, "It's an old house. It makes these telltale sounds."

Lauren lifted her chin. "Then?"

He turned to her. "I grabbed the bear spray. I saw the doorknob turning. The door opened. I sprayed him in the face, the gun went off, he fell down, started screaming that he was going to 'fucking kill me'. A bullet went past my face. I stood up, grabbed the toilet tank lid, hit him over the head, called 911. Then I went outside, sat on the front sidewalk until the cops came."

Lauren asked, "You're a hiker?"

"Sometimes." Dave glanced out the window as an ambulance pulled up in the emergency garage.

Lauren pointed at him with her finger. "What kind of hiking do you do?"

He looked at her, hesitated before replying. "I go up to Banff or Kananaskis."

"Ever see any bears?"

"No."

Lauren used her thumb and forefinger to play with the silver hoop earring in her right earlobe. "When did you buy the bear spray?"

"Couple of years ago."

Lauren nodded. "Two, three, four years?"

"Why are you asking about the fucking bear spray? The asshole was going to kill me. He had a gun! I have a right to defend myself."

Nigel asked, "Why would someone want to kill you?"

Dave rubbed his palms on his thighs. "No idea."

Lauren asked, "What do Canadian National Investors Group and Wright Trust Financial have to do with the attempt on your life?"

"Nothing."

Lauren frowned, noticing the sweat along Dave's hairline.

He shook his head. "I'm tired. I just want to go home."

Nigel shook his head. "Our forensics unit is going to be working at your place for a while yet. You won't be able to get much rest there."

"I've got a friend I can stay with."

Lauren locked her fingers around her knee. "Initially, the evidence supports your claim of self-defence." She paused, looking at Dave. "I'm just not sure why you are lying to us about the bear spray."

Nigel leaned forward.

Dave wiped his T-shirt across his forehead. "How do you know that?"

"I checked the manufacturer's code on the bottom of the can. It left the factory on January eighth of this year."

He looked out the window. "What do you want from me?"

"I think you're afraid. If that's the case, who are you afraid of?"

David continued looking outside. "They killed Martina."

"Tell us about Martina," Nigel said.

David looked at Nigel, Lauren and back out the window. "I'm fucked."

Nigel leaned in.

"Who is Martina?"

David continued looking out the window.

Nigel needs to back off. "Sir, you need to…"

Nigel said, "Who are they?"

Lauren said, "Nigel, please…"

Nigel said, "Look at me!"

Lauren reached over, put her hand on Nigel's shoulder, squeezing hard with her thumb and forefinger. "I need to talk to you outside."

Her boss's eyes were black with rage. "What?"

She stood up, wincing from a memory of her mother, her eyes enraged as he talked with the RCMP officer at the detachment in Kenton the night Lauren was arrested.

"Outside." Lauren walked to the door, holding it open for him.

The hallway was the same shade of pee as the room. Nigel worked his right arm, moving the shoulder as she closed the door.

He asked, "What the hell?"

"He needs a lawyer."

"What do you mean? He was ready to talk." Nigel kept his voice low because a man with a plastic leg cast was passing on crutches.

"He needs a lawyer. I checked out Wright Trust Financial and Canadian National Investors Group. Both are based here. Both were named in the Paradise Papers but managed to weasel their way out of the scandal with a little help from the PMO. The Prime Minister lost the last election over it. Remember?"

Nigel nodded. "Okay?"

"I checked the serial number on the Ruger. It was bought in Georgia. I also checked the ID on the dead guy's rental car. It's fake. My gut and the evidence are saying we may be able to connect the killer to WTF and CNIG. If that's the case, then Singer needs us to protect him. The longer we hold onto him, the safer he is. And he needs a lawyer for his own protection. We need a lawyer here so these assholes can't wiggle their way out of this one. That is, if I'm right."

Nigel's eyebrows lifted as he rubbed his collarbone. "You're from Kenton, Saskatchewan, right?" He looked at her long fingers and tiger paw palms.

"Yes. My dad and mom ran a farm outside of town."

"You learned that from your dad?" He rolled his shoulder.

Lauren smiled. "No. Mom taught me that one."

He put his nose a centimetre from hers. "Don't ever do that again. My dad used to do that to me."

"What would you suggest I do instead?"

Nigel's eyebrows lifted, ploughing furrows in his forehead. "Tell me to shut up."

The note taped to Lane's third floor condo door was pale blue with words spaced exactly.

Dear 305 Resident,
Your car is parked precisely 3.5 centimetres left of centre in your underground parking space. This creates an untenable situation for me as getting in and out of my vehicle is made more difficult. I take great pride in maintaining and preserving my Porsche. Rectify the situation by being more careful while parking your vehicle.

Also, it has come to the attention of some residents that you have a reputation for traipsing around your unit in the nude. Your reflection can be seen clearly in the mirror in your front room through a gap in the curtains. This is an unpleasant situation for your neighbours. Rectify this situation as well.
Sincerely,
The Condo Board

Lane peeled the note off the door before opening and closing it, kicking off his shoes, stuffing the note inside the red file with the others, all the while on mental autopilot. He set his keys next to the file, looking left.

Below the mirror, atop the ledge over the gas fireplace were pictures of him, Arthur and family on their wedding day. The sun reflected on the Bow River under a clear blue prairie sky. Flower girl Ella sat in a red wagon. Indy wore a white shirt, black vest and shorts. Dan and Christine stood behind the kids, with Matt and Alexandra beside them and next to Dan's sister Linda. Sitting out front, Arthur leaned his head against Lane's shoulder.

Lane looked away from the image and out the window to Kensington Road. He remembered talking with Arthur about moving to Kensington someday. They both enjoyed the district's eclectic blend of old, new, odd, restaurants, coffee and relaxed attitude.

He sighed, turning, heading for the bedroom, hoping for the elusive oblivion of sleep.

Tommy Pham wore a navy blue suit, electric blue tie and a double chin while sitting with fingers interlaced across the table from Nigel and Lauren. "How is our friend, Paul?"

Nigel looked out the window at downtown Calgary – its

towering office buildings dwarfed by a Rocky Mountain background. "I haven't seen him for about a month."

Tommy waited. Lauren studied the pair of them. *Aren't we supposed to be here about Dave Singer?*

Nigel faced Tommy. "He moved closer to downtown."

"Uncle Tran has been asking about Paul." Tommy ran his palm down his tie.

"So has Anna. She's worried about him too. Want me to ask Lori? She's been keeping tabs on him."

"The executive assistant to the chief of police?"

Nigel nodded. "That's correct."

I wish there'd been more time to powder my nose. Lauren's fingers tapped the tabletop. "About Mr. Singer. We have an urgent request."

Tommy smiled.

"My associate will be here in a moment." He tucked his tie in his belt. "You knew Detective Paul Lane?"

Lauren put her hands under the table. "I met him a couple of times as part of an investigation."

Tommy turned his hands palms up. "You do not think it is important to show concern for those who have made your life better?"

He's a lawyer. Don't lose your temper. He argues and provokes for a living. "I think it's important to protect a man whose life is at risk at this moment."

Tommy nodded, lifting his chin at the crisp knock on the door.

A lean, dark-haired woman wearing glasses, a navy blue pantsuit, black tie and white blouse entered.

Lauren noticed she was wearing a pair of orange running shoes and thought, *She is anywhere between thirteen and thirty. This could be interesting.*

She sat down next to Lauren and across from Tommy who said, "This is Evelyn Hua. She has agreed to listen to your proposal regarding Mr. Singer." He pointed at Nigel. "This is Detective Li." He turned to Lauren. "Detective Jackson."

Evelyn nodded.

Nigel said, "We have a complicated situation. We believe –" he glanced at Lauren "– and the evidence indicates that David Singer was targeted, managed to kill his attacker and now is in our custody. Lauren thinks, and I agree, it's in all of our best interests if Singer has legal representation before we interrogate him to find out why he was targeted."

Tommy asked, "Any indications of who targeted him?"

Nigel said, "We are in the initial stages of the investigation and we have some leads."

Tommy tapped the desk with his forefinger. "You understand that no part of this conversation will leave this room."

Lauren watched as Evelyn pushed back the cuticles of her right fingernails with the eraser at the end of a pencil.

Mom always taught me if the boys in the room start to talk as if you aren't there, then it's your job to make 'em notice. She leaned left, bringing her right cheek up off the seat. The fart was loud, a protracted cackling. She turned to her superior and said, "Oh, excuse me. Boss?"

Evelyn looked up, a smile appearing, then disappearing.

Tommy leaned back, startled.

Nigel turned to Lauren, his eyebrows working at getting together while his face reddened.

Lauren said, "The dead man at the scene has yet to be identified. He was carrying a silenced, unregistered handgun. Singer mentioned a friend of his named Martina who he says was killed. That's why I believe he was expecting the killer. Singer purchased a can of bear spray to protect himself. We are attempting to find out more about Martina. Early indications are there may be a connection with Canadian National Investors' Group and Wright Trust Financial. Singer needs a lawyer to protect his interests and allow us to gather as much information as possible about the involvement of CNIG and WTF so we can find out who hired the killer."

Evelyn said, "I'll take it. When can I meet with Singer?"

"How about tomorrow morning at 9 am?" Lauren pulled her phone out. "If you give me your number I can text the address."

Both of them turned as Tommy inhaled, slapping the table with his palm. His face was red, his eyes watering.

Oh no! He's having a heart attack.

Laughter jumped out of him. He pointed at Lauren. "You played us!"

Lauren smiled, feeling the rush of red to her cheeks.

CHAPTER 2

Lane woke to the clatter of a diesel engine wheezing and farting as it pulled away from the lights on Kensington Road. He lifted the covers, sat up, pulling on shorts and a T-shirt, then walked down the hallway and into the kitchen.

While waiting for the espresso machine to heat up, he peeled and ate a banana before taking one of the little white pills the doctor had prescribed. Apparently, Citalopram had something to do with serotonin and was supposed to ease the depression.

He contemplated the efficacy of serotonin while grinding coffee beans, steaming milk, adding espresso. He stood at the island, his eyes falling on the folder of letters. *What would Arthur say to the head of the condo board?*

Nigel sat in the front room in his red leather easy chair. His daughter, her black hair wild and curly, slept on his chest, drooling onto his T-shirt.

His phone danced on the arm of the chair. He read the face, seeing it was the office of the chief calling. He picked up the phone with his left hand, using his thumb to answer, whispering, "Nigel Li."

"This a bad time?" Lori asked, adopting his quiet tone.

"Natalie and I are having some quiet time, she's asleep. Anna is asleep."

"Want me to call back?"

"It's okay. What's up?" He listened to Natalie's breathing, hoping she wouldn't stir.

"There was a call to Lane's address. A complaint about indecent exposure."

He frowned. "What? You sure?"

"A unit is there right now. Thought you'd want to know. Do you have any idea where he goes for coffee these days?"

"I'll do some checking." He looked out the front window, seeing if the stroller was on the veranda.

"I'll contact the officers after they finish their interview, then get back to you." Lori hung up.

Jackson sat at her computer, searching for background on Wright Trust Financial. Each time a name appeared, no matter how remote the connection, she wrote it in a yellow lined notebook. Then she researched each name, making sketches and more notes, creating a detailed map of the company, its people and their dealings.

She leaned back in her chair, lifting her arms, stretching muscles, looking at the white ceiling tiles. Her phone rang. She leaned forward, recognizing the name. "What's up Hashir?"

"Roland Wilson is our dead guy with the silenced handgun."

Lauren picked up a pencil, added the name in her notebook. "Where did you find him?"

"Armed Forces. He was in the reserves for a couple of years in Ontario. Even trained for three weeks at Wainwright. He worked at a Ford dealership in Toronto as a parts guy. Owns a two-million-dollar home. Divorced five years ago. Several reports of domestic abuse with no charges."

"Did you talk with the ex?"

"Not yet. Tracking her down. She moved to Victoria."

"Getting as far away from Roland as possible?"

Hashir took a breath. "I'll let you know if I find her."

Brenda sat sipping a low fat, soy chai latte. She wore a floral housecoat from the Reitman's spring collection, facing her laptop, watching a YYC News video.

The neighbours' early 20th Century sandstone filled her kitchen window. She moved her fingers on the track pad, freezing the image of a bungalow bordered by yellow tape, putting it next to an image she'd cut from Google Earth, checking the address on her burner phone with the number of the house in the news video.

"Fuck!"

Lane opened the door to Hexagon, smiled back at Randy's round smiling face. The barista asked, "The usual?"

Lane nodded before frowning when Randy lifted his eyebrows, leaning his head to the left. Lane spotted Lori and Nigel sitting at the long table sipping their drinks and waiting. Natalie struggled in the stroller next to Nigel. Lori lifted her eyebrows, smiling, standing, moving toward him, hugging him around the shoulders and resting her head against him.

"Been a while," she said, before leaning away, holding his elbows, her blue eyes taking him in. "You've lost weight."

Black-haired, freckle-faced Nigel stood, shaking Lane's hand, then embracing him. He smelled of sour milk and aftershave.

"Sit down with us," Nigel said.

Lane thought, *I wonder if they heard about this morning?*

Lori sat at the head of the table with the men on either side of her.

Might just as well get right to it. "What's up?"

Lori smiled without looking at Nigel. "The kids are good?"

Lane nodded. "Yours?"

"Driving me crazy but good." Lori patted Nigel on the shoulder of his blue shirt. "And it looks like little Natalie christened our friend this morning."

Nigel looked at the white stain on the shoulder of his purple T-shirt. "I thought I got all of it."

Lori laughed, wrinkling her nose before turning to Lane. "I hear you had visitors this morning."

Lane tried unsuccessfully not to blush, feeling the heat starting at the tips of his ears, shrugging. "The condo board is pissing me off. I get these notes taped to my door telling me how to park and to keep my drapes closed. I started to think about Arthur and how he would have reacted, so I stripped down, did a few downward dogs. Then some sun salutations and tree poses."

He closed his mouth, realizing he'd said more than he should.

Lori laughed out loud.

Randy said, "Mochaccino."

Nigel asked, "Want another?"

Lori shook her head. "You go ahead."

Nigel stood, returning with Lane's mochaccino, setting it on the table, before ordering a second latte.

Lori touched Lane's forearm. "I haven't seen you for a while. Been keeping tabs. A friend let me know about this morning's call, so we decided to get some coffee."

He reached for his mocha with his free hand, feeling close to tears. "Good to see you."

"To put your mind at ease, your neighbour made the

mistake of videotaping you on his cell phone."

"Did he put it online?"

She rubbed his shoulder. "No time. He thought it would prove you guilty of indecent exposure. Instead, the officers asked for the phone as evidence to charge him with invasion of privacy. Apparently, the guy went off on them, threw the phone at one officer, spat at the other and was arrested. He's in lock up as we speak."

Nigel sat back down.

Lane shrugged. "How is Anna?"

Nigel lifted his empty coffee cup. "Anna is tired. We are adjusting to this new normal." He looked left at his daughter, seeing her face turning red.

Lori looked at Lane. "You the same way?"

"How do you mean?"

"Always checking to see if the little ones are safe?"

Lane smiled, nodding. "Alexandra is pregnant."

Lori leaned forward. "When's she due?"

"Yesterday."

She lifted her coffee. "You dropped off the radar after the funeral."

He shrugged.

A pungent aroma rose up from Natalie. Nigel put his latte down, picking her up.

"Anna talked to Christine. She said they are worried about you."

Lane looked at the wall. "I'm fine."

Lori shook her head. "Bullshit. You forget how well I know you. You're hiding inside that shell again."

An unfamiliar emotion bubbled from somewhere under his ribs. "What do you know about it?"

Lori leaned closer, pointing her finger, touching his nose. "I know you. You're shutting yourself off; insulating yourself." She pointed at Nigel then herself. "It's our business to know."

Nigel nodded, releasing Natalie's straps.

Lane shrugged. "I always felt safe with Arthur around. This

morning I was thinking about how Arthur would fight the bully neighbour." *Why are you explaining?*

Lori smiled.

"Yes, that yoga move had Arthur written all over it. I miss him."

Lane nodded, wiping his eyes with his palm. "We had plans for our retirement."

Nigel said, "Shit happens," reaching for the diaper bag.

Lori blanched, looking sideways at Nigel. Her eyes wide, mouth open.

Lane inhaled, barking as he exhaled. Leaning forward then back, laughing 'til the tears came.

Hashir Wajdan squeezed his frame into an office chair sitting next to Lauren Jackson at the conference room table. "I may have found something when I was checking the database. Interpol has this photograph..." he opened his laptop, turning it so she could see the image, "...of a suspect in the murder of a Zurich CEO."

Lauren studied the side view of a man in a ball cap waiting at an elevator. "It could be Wilson. Does the height and weight match?"

Hashir nodded. "Yes. Toronto police are checking his whereabouts at the time. They are also in the process of obtaining a search warrant for his apartment."

Lauren sketched and wrote as they talked. "Anything new on WTF or the others?"

Hashir turned the laptop to face him, tapping a key. "That's the thing. The Zurich CEO, his name was Demarco, he was about to blow the whistle on investment firms, including WTF and CNIG. When I called Zurich, they wanted us to share information with them. They are working to solve the Demarco murder and asked for Wilson's DNA results. They have what they believe to be sample from the killer."

"What kind of sample?"

"From the inside of a rubber glove left near where the suspect was photographed."

Lauren tapped the face of her phone. "These pictures are from David Singer's home." She manipulated the image with thumb and forefinger, enlarging a sticky note from the wall. "He had these near his computer screens."

Hashir leaned in, reading the image. "WTF and CNIG. Interesting."

"We are going to interview Singer with his lawyer tomorrow morning."

Hashir leaned back. "I thought you and the boss were doing the interview."

She shook her head. "He texted me earlier. He wants you on this. We need to gather as much information as possible before then. Especially about the WTF/CNIG connection, if it has any relevance of course."

He smiled. "You think it's relevant and so do I."

Brenda sniffed one armpit, then the other, repeating the process three more times. Freddy Wright wasn't taking her calls anymore. His son Colin was. She considered the Oedipal implications of the son's willingness to communicate. She closed her eyes, concentrating instead on Colin's attractions to risk and self-help schtick, opening her eyes, reaching for her phone. Colin answered after the first ring. *Good, he's anxious.*

"Hey Colin." *Keep it calm, soothing.* "How are things at your end?"

"The old man is freaking out. He saw the news and is in panic mode. He thinks this is all about to blow up in his face like the PMO scandal."

"This may be an opportunity..." *The hook is baited.* "For us."

"You mean this could divert attention away from us instead of at us?"

"I was thinking of something a little different, actually." *He's closer now, just let him ask the questions.*

"Okay? We can make money on this?"

Set the hook. "We just focus on the problem. We work for people who want to protect their money. Reputations are important but money is their primary focus. We show them how this uncertainty is an opportunity for them."

"And?"

"Maybe it's time for some restructuring, a convenient scapegoat, some public bloodletting. Then back to business as usual with improved investor confidence, which means protecting assets and making money for the clients. And in turn, we continue to make progress." *Did I oversell it?*

"Okay, let's hear the plan."

CHAPTER 3

The walls were Brazilian ebony. Lauren knew this because a brass wall plaque proclaimed the wood's origins. It was on the wall behind the metre wide and 20 centimetre thick polished table on which the torso of Freddy Wright rested – a dead cowboy with comb-over stretching for the carpet. The remainder of the seventy-year-old legendary entrepreneur, along with his alligator skin cowboy boots, was on top of the table.

Hashir asked, "How come we were called on this one? Looks like natural causes."

"The death nurse smelled insulin. She checked around." Lauren looked left at the open door to the private washroom. "No needle or insulin in the fridge. She thought it best if we took a look. Besides, Wright was on the boards of CNIG and WTF. When Nigel heard, he called us in."

She walked over to the washroom, putting her gloved hands on either side of the frame, leaning in, seeing the vomit on the walls and floor. She leaned back, lifting her chin at Hashir, eyes pointing to the office door. "The ME is going to have to check for any needle marks or bruising on the body." She looked down the hallway leading to the elevators. "You

want to check with security and see if they have any video?"
She reached in her pocket for the phone. "I'll wait for the
forensics team."

Lane walked off the elevator into the condo's underground
parking. His steps echoed along the concrete foundation walls.
He saw the empty parking spot next to his blue Ford Edge, then
the scratch in the paint reaching from taillight to headlight on
the passenger side. He looked around for the Porsche then
followed the scratch around his vehicle.

He stopped at the driver's door, reaching for his phone,
finding the number for his insurance company.

Hashir's hair was brushed and he looked none the worse for
wear. Lauren had done her best, but doubted she looked as
fresh as he did. Both had worked through the night, taking
time for 30 minute naps on the sleeping bags stowed in the
bottom drawers of their desks. Hashir checked the face of his
phone.

Lauren asked, "Kids okay?"

He nodded. "Sanjiv got them all off to school."

The black door of the white interview room opened.
Evelyn Hua poked her head in. She had her black hair tied back
in a ponytail, wore blue-framed glasses red blouse, black
palazzo pants and red boots. She held her briefcase in her left,
gesturing for David Singer to enter the room. His black hair
was neatly and freshly trimmed. He wore a white shirt, grey
dress pants and blue running shoes.

Lauren thought, *Bet Evelyn did your clothes shopping.*

Evelyn held out a chair for Singer, putting her briefcase

beside her as she sat.

"My client has agreed to make a statement and to answer your questions as long as the following conditions are signed." She pulled a folder from her briefcase, setting it on the table, opening it, sliding a two-page stapled document to Lauren.

Hashir stood up, taking the document with him before exiting the room.

Lauren said, "It will be reviewed by my superiors who will get right back to us. Nigel and the crown prosecutor will be going over the conditions, so it's my job to keep things light."

She turned to Singer whose brown eyes had gone from shocked to calculating, perhaps even a bit confident. "You look better today. Evelyn is taking good care of you."

He looked at Evelyn before nodding. "Yes."

Lauren pulled a file from her briefcase, setting it on the table without opening it.

Singer asked, "How long will they be?"

She inhaled, watching Evelyn reading a message on her phone. "Not sure. Shouldn't be long."

The door opened, Hashir stepping in, closing the door, setting the document on the table in front of Evelyn. "We've agreed to every stipulation except the last. If we discover Mr. Singer was involved in the murder of Martina Villanova, then the agreement will be null and void." He smiled at Lauren. "Nigel told me I had to say that."

"They killed Martina, not me." Singer sat erect.

Evelyn put her hand on Singer's arm as she perused both pages of the document, checking the date, the signatures and the handwritten note at the bottom of the last page. "Agreed." She checked the face of her phone, tapping the timer. "You have 60 minutes for the initial interview."

Lauren thought, *Enough of this.* She set her phone at the exact centre of the table. "This conversation is being recorded. Detectives Hashir and Jackson are present along with David Singer and his lawyer Evelyn Hua. Mr. Singer, you agreed to talk about Wright Trust Financial and Canadian National

Investors Group known respectively as WTF and CNIG?"

Singer nodded, glancing at the phone before saying, "Yes."

Lauren waited. She sensed Hashir leaning across the table, closing the distance between he and Singer by a centimetre or two.

"I met Martina Villanova for the first time in Cabos San Lucas, Mexico. She was writing for FresaLeaks and got me interested." Singer rubbed his right shoulder with his left palm.

Lauren waited, determined to let Singer talk.

"After I came home, I followed some leads she gave me about WTF and CNIG. She discovered how some wealthy individuals in Mexico, the US and Canada were avoiding paying taxes. She obtained copies of communications between Freddy Wright and high-ranking members at the PMO about a year ago. I helped leak the information. The resulting scandal ultimately resulted in the defeat of the government."

"By PMO you are referring the Prime Minister's Office in Ottawa?"

"Correct. More recently we have been working on the release of documents revealing similar connections between high ranking former members of the U.S. presidential staff and other wealthy members of the Mexican government."

"How did you find out Martina had been killed?"

"We were FaceTiming. She was shot in front of me."

"Then?"

"I went out and bought some bear spray and carried it with me wherever." He looked at the ceiling, inhaling deeply. "I live in an old house. I heard the floorboards creaking when that guy came inside."

Lauren asked, "Did the shooter say anything?"

"He said, `This is what happens when you piss off powerful people.' Then he opened the door. I hit him with the spray. The gun went off. I dropped the spray, grabbed the lid off the toilet and hit him over the head."

"What was his position when you hit him?"

Singer looked at the floor. "He was on his knees, reaching

for his gun."

"Did he say anything?"

"'I'm gonna kill you, you motherfucker.' I hit him again, then called 9-1-1."

Lauren checked her notes. "What were you and Martina working on prior to the attacks?"

Singer glanced at Evelyn who tapped her index finger once on the table. "We discovered correspondence between Freddy Wright and the 45s."

Lauren looked at Hashir, who said, "Freddy Wright is dead."

Evelyn tapped her index finger twice on the table. "This interview is concluded." She stood up, taking her client by the arm, leaving the room.

Baker Park was situated on the north side of the Bow River, crisscrossed with paved trails.

Brenda wore a form-fitting yoga T-shirt and pants as agreed upon, lifting her bike helmet off, pushing fingers through her brown bob, feeling the sweat along her hairline. She'd borrowed the bike from the rack in the basement of her condo. Her legs felt like rubber as she leaned it against the bench facing the river.

She looked west as semis hummed over Stoney Bridge. She sat down at the far end of the bench. A woman walked mismatched dogs to her left and beyond that, a lone jogger wore a bright blue top and black shorts.

Brenda's eyes went back and forth from the jogger to the dog walker, checking for any indication the two recognized one another. The jogger passed the woman, closing the distance, stopping ten metres away. He turned a full 360 degrees before walking up to Brenda and taking the other end of the bench.

Colin Wright's salt and pepper hair clung to his forehead,

his trim six-foot-two frame wrapped in Spandex. "I told them I needed a run. The family is in the middle of contacting relatives and planning his funeral." He glanced at his wrist. "We've only got a few minutes."

Interesting, he calls his family 'the family' as if he is somehow separate. Brenda decided to take control. "Let's clear one thing up, I had nothing to do with your father's death."

Colin turned to face her, studying her with his grey eyes. "I didn't kill him."

She leaned back, sizing him up, opening her mouth and closing it, thinking about an appropriate response, finding none.

"Look." He put his hands on his knees, gazing out over the river. "Yes, I wanted him out of the family business. Yes, he and I didn't get along. But no, I didn't kill him. I was in Canmore last night. The police have already come to talk with me and are verifying my alibi."

"That only proves you weren't there, and you didn't do the killing yourself."

"Okay." He turned to face her, reading her expression. "You can believe me or not. The fact is I didn't kill Freddy, didn't have him killed and–if you had nothing to do with it either–then we have a bigger problem."

Brenda looked across the river. *Or some negotiating to do.*

Lauren stood facing the wall beside her desk with her right foot tucked up next to her thigh, eyes focused on a pink sticky note with a dot in the middle. She concentrated on her breathing as she balanced in tree pose, focusing her mind while clearing it of extraneous thoughts and distractions.

Just breathe, think of nothing else.

Her phone rang.

Just breathe!

A second ring. She glanced at the phone, seeing Hashir's name as she lost her balance, set her right foot on the floor, and reached for the phone. "Jackson."

"You were right, there is evidence of bruising just below and to the right of Wright's navel. Also, his medical records indicate no history of diabetes or prescribed use of insulin. The ME says something was injected into Wright's abdomen. Because insulin is a naturally occurring substance, it will be difficult to prove. The ME also said that he will do a DNA test on the vomit in Wright's bathroom to see if it's a match. Finally, he said that vomiting is symptomatic of an insulin overdose."

Lauren looked at her notebook, bringing her thoughts back to the case. "Sugar called 30 minutes ago. He and the office security found three cameras in the underground parking lot were coated with a clear petroleum product."

"So we have indications of tampering but no clear images and little in the way of proof."

"So far."

"The ME is pretty much done here. I should be back at the office in half an hour." Hashir hung up.

"What did they say about your car?" Christine sat in her backyard watching Ella and Indy wrestling with their Uncle Matt. Lane sat in between her and the pregnant-for-ten-months Alexandra, who sipped water from a glass resting atop her belly.

Lane shrugged. "I had to report it to the CPS because the damage was over $1,000, so it all got very involved. I've got an appointment next week and a loaner."

"Oohh!" Alexandra lifted her water glass.

"How's our kicker doing?" Christine leaned forward to better see her sister.

"That was a good one. This little guy is making it hard for

me to get any sleep." Alexandra pointed her glass at Lane. "You don't seem too upset about the damage to your car."

"Arthur called that kind of thing a first world problem. Not worth worrying about. I know who did it. He wasn't very clever about it. The security cameras recorded him doing the damage. Copies of the video were sent to the police, insurance company and condo board. The whole mess will keep my OCD neighbour busy for the next while."

They watched as Indy climbed Matt's back, grabbing him by the collar, rocking back and forth on 'Uncle Horse.' Ella came from a different angle, crawling under the bridge made by Matt's hands and knees.

Christine said, "Gentle with Uncle Matt, you two."

Alexandra sipped water. "My bladder must be the size of a shot glass by now." She set the glass on the glass-topped table, shifting her weight forward, pulling herself to her feet. "Be right back."

Lane watched Ella stand up and slap Matt across the hindquarters. He bucked, Indy lost his balance, landing face first in the grass. There was a collective intake of breath.

Indy got to hands and knees, spitting grass, snot and a howl. Christine launched herself out of her chair. Matt lifted Indy up who reached for his mother.

Lane felt a vibration in his shirt pocket. Christine wrapped her sobbing son around her neck. Matt rubbed Indy's back. Lane picked up Ella. She touched his chest as his phone vibrated again.

Christine wiped Indy's nose with a tissue.

Ella unbuttoned Lane's shirt pocket, handing him his phone. He touched the face with his thumb, reading a text message:

It has been some time since you visited Mexico. I was wondering if you would be interested in another vacation. There is a matter of interest to your country and mine requiring your particular skill set. If you are willing, please advise. Andreas Rodriguez.

"What?" Christine asked.

Lane lifted his head to see all eyes, including Indy's on him. Ella took the phone from Lane's hand, giving it to Christine who read the message before handing it to Matt.

Christine shook her head. "General Rodriguez locked you and Nigel up in Cancun, right?"

Lane shrugged, turning to Ella who was set to put a wet finger in his ear. He took her hand. *Nothing stays secret for very long around here.*

Matt said, "Almost got you killed."

Christine jumped in. "Messed up Nigel and Anna's wedding. It's like legendary. Didn't a video of you and Nigel being marched off by armed guards go viral?"

Alexandra stepped out the door, clutching her abdomen with one hand and the arm of the chair with the other.

Indy sniffed, twitching his nose, pointing.

"Grass up there."

Alexandra pushed her black hair back, taking a slow breath. "I think my water just broke."

Nigel sat in his living room. The evening sun painted the walls a more vivid version of themselves. His daughter was tucked against his chest. He heard the gentle sound of her breathing. Anna was on the couch, elbow covering her eyes, snoring after hours of chasing Natalie around the park.

Nigel waited for the gentle rise and fall of both their chests, then his phone danced on the arm of the easy chair. He leaned forward, standing, checking the number, walking into the kitchen. "Twice in one week? How are you Lori?"

"Shitty, thanks for asking."

He looked out the back window at their apple tree. "Okay?"

"The Chief wants you to contact Paul Lane about going to

Mexico with Jackson."

"Lane? You're kidding right?"

"No. No kidding, sweetie. I tried to talk her out of it, but this comes from someone high up in CSIS or Ottawa. It's hard to tell which."

"What's goin' on?"

"This Wright murder and hired assassin thing has people spooked. I don't know. It looks like Wright was murdered but there is precious little evidence. Now somebody high up in the Mexican government knows about the attempt on Singer and the death of Wright. They believe it's all linked to the murder of Martina Villanova and connected to the 45s."

"How do CSIS and the Mexicans know so much about what's going on here?"

"As far as I can tell the Chief has been receiving calls about our investigation since this afternoon. After supper, the calls from Ottawa have become more frequent. I tried to tell her Lane was still grieving and he'd done enough, but she told me to ask anyway."

Nigel remembered the last time he'd seen his friend and mentor, how Lane had lost weight and seemed to be fading, leaking whatever joy he'd once gotten from life. "What was your impression of Lane when we saw him?"

"Like he's lost interest in food, life, coffee. He used to have this intensity and it's gone."

"Think putting him in the middle of something like this will help him find his way back?"

Lori laughed. It was a dry, humourless sound. "Or put him in the ground."

"The last time we got paired up with the Mexicans we came within centimetres of eating an RPG."

"I tried to tell that to the Chief. She still wants you to ask."

Nigel felt Anna's hand on his shoulder. She touched his cheek, then asked, "What's up?"

He covered the phone and said, "They want Lane back."

Anna shook her head, smiling. "Good luck with that! I

wouldn't want to be the one who tries to sell it to Christine. She's a tiger and a grizzly all rolled up into one protective mama."

Saturday, May 6

CHAPTER 4

Nigel knocked on the conference room door, opening it to find Lauren's notebooks and laptop spread out over half the table. She sat cross-legged on the floor, eyes closed, palms on her knees.

"What's up boss?"

Nigel waited for her to open her eyes. "Ever heard of a place called Todos Santos?"

She opened one eye. "All Saints?"

"That's what it means. You know where it is?"

"Baja, California."

Nigel closed the door behind him. "Ever been there?"

She shook her head. "Nope."

"You're gonna need summer clothes."

"Why me, and what's Todos Santos got to do with the case I'm working on?"

Nigel shrugged. "You speak Spanish and you and Lane have been asked to go there to learn what the Mexicans know about this case."

"I thought Lane was retired."

He sat down as she stood. "Some folks from Ottawa think otherwise."

Lauren studied Nigel's expression. "What aren't you telling

Lane woke to the sound of hissing steam and the soothing scent of espresso. He pushed himself to sitting, putting his feet on the floor, stretching the kinks out of his back. He stood up, tugging at the knees of his pants before walking to Christine and Dan's kitchen.

Dan faced the espresso machine and said, "Bet you want a coffee."

"That would be nice." Lane pulled out a kitchen chair and sat at the table. "Alexandra okay?"

"Sorry, nobody told you. I got to the hospital about two in the morning. Half an hour later the baby was born."

"Everybody okay?" He watched as Dan finished steaming the milk.

Dan added milk to the espresso. "Everybody's good including Karen. She's a doll with lots of black hair. Matt can't take his eyes off her. Christine is thrilled to be an aunt."

Lane nodded, smiling. "That is good news."

Dan set one cup in front of Lane and the other across the table where he sat. "Thanks for looking after the kids last night."

"Watched a movie, ate some popcorn, then they fell asleep." He looked over his shoulder toward the living room. "Okay if I borrow your phone charger? Mine's dead."

"Nope. We're gonna have breakfast first." Dan put his hands on the table, preparing to stand. "Christine got a call from Lori last night. She's been trying to get in touch with you. Something about Ottawa wanting you to go back to Mexico. After five calls, Christine agreed to let Lori meet you here." He pointed at his kitchen table. "Christine made me promise to make you breakfast and–" he looked at his watch "–wake her up half an hour before Lori gets here." He stood.

"What's goin' on?" Lane stared at his coffee, flashing back

to the trail of an RPG illuminating the inside of an armoured vehicle. He shivered at the impact of the shock wave.

Dan shrugged. "Apparently it's something big and Lori had to do a lot of convincing before Christine would let her know where you are."

"I don't know why she thinks she has to look after me." Lane looked out the window at the backyard and its blue and red blossoms.

"She loves you."

Lane's mouth and brain refused to connect. He shrugged.

Indy woke up when the smell of toasted bagels filled the kitchen. He came downstairs wearing a red T-shirt and grey pajama bottoms.

Lane asked, "Want some bagel?"

Indy walked over to the table, sitting on the bench at the end, resting on his elbows as Dan set a plate of bagels in front of him. Lane cut the halved bagels into quarters. Indy picked one up and began eating while Dan brewed a second latte for himself and Lane.

Christine arrived downstairs minutes later, hugging her son around the shoulders, kissing her husband, reaching for her phone. "Indy, want to see what your new cousin looks like?"

Ella joined them.

Indy played a game on his iPod while Ella sat on her father's lap writing invites to her birthday. It was one of her favourite activities. She practiced it at least once every week.

Christine got up, putting her phone in front of Indy's face. "Your new cousin."

Indy said, "Cute," then went back to his game.

Lori arrived in the middle of it all, almost 60 minutes later. Lane saw her through the living room window as she stepped up to the front door. As always, her blonde hair was cut shoulder length. Lane frowned when he saw the brown-haired woman next to her. She was taller, slender, wore a light blue blouse and navy blazer. He recognized her as a homicide detective he'd met a few years ago during the floods.

Christine opened the door, "Hey Lori," hugging her close. "You know he's done enough, right?"

Lori stepped inside, kicking off pumps. "I know."

Lane got up, hugging his old friend. "Come and sit down."

Christine asked, "Who's this?"

Lori said, "Lauren Jackson," motioning for her to come inside.

Christine got them settled in the front room, Dan took coffee orders, Indy concentrated on his game and Ella tucked herself in beside Christine on the easy chair. Lane sat down beside Indy, putting his arm around the boy's shoulders. Lauren and Lori sat in front of the window.

Lori said, "Congratulations on the new baby. How are mom and daughter doing?"

Christine shook her head. "They're fine. Waiting to go home this afternoon. I think this plan involving my uncle is a bad idea."

Lane noted Christine's use of the possessive and smiled. *And the conversation has just started.* He felt something unusual stirring, trying and failing to identify the emotion.

Lori sipped her tea, setting the cup down on a coaster.

"Ottawa is asking for Lane. It's about this case Lauren has been investigating. Apparently, it has international implications."

Christine pointed at Lauren. "What do you say?"

Lauren looked at the oak floor before staring Christine down. "It's early stages yet, so we're gathering information on two and possibly three violent deaths."

"That's the best you can do?" Christine leaned forward, Ella hanging onto her arm. "Generalities and euphemisms aren't going to cut it here."

Dan said, "We could use more specifics." He turned to Lauren. "Do you know what happened to Matt?"

Lauren nodded. "Kidnapped. Escaped. Saved the former Chief's daughter in the process." She looked at Lori who waited, then Lauren turned to Christine. "Okay then. You sure you want the kids to hear this?"

Indy said, "Yes."

Christine said, "Kids go upstairs."

Ella said, "No."

"Just keep it a little vague," said Lane and held up a thumb and forefinger with about a millimetre between.

Lauren drained her espresso, momentarily examining the fine grains at the bottom. "It looks like a tax evasion scheme has been operating, at least in part, out of Calgary and Mexico City. It also appears that the recent attempt on a life in the southwest was related to leaked information about the same money scheme. The leaks have shone an intense light on wealthy North Americans. At least one of them has taken out contracts to turn the spotlight off." She looked at Lane. "An old acquaintance of yours has asked for you to accompany me to Mexico to investigate the people responsible."

"Can you speak Spanish?" Indy asked without looking up from the game.

"Yes. I'm fluent." Lauren smiled, briefly.

"Pruébalo," Indy said.

"¿Por qué estás rompiendo las pelotas?" Lauren cocked one eye at Indy.

He lifted his head, shocking everyone when he started laughing.

Ella said, "Women don't have balls!"

Lauren smiled at Christine. "Your kids know Spanish!"

She nodded. "They go to a Spanish immersion school and my sister has been teaching them some on the side." She lifted Ella, setting her to the other side, looking at Lori. "Why did the Chief send you here?"

Lori looked right back and said, "She's worried about her career. The guys in Ottawa want Lane, and she wants to keep the guys in Ottawa happy so she can climb the ladder to Central Canada."

"I don't care what Ottawa wants or what Mexico wants or

what Wright and his buddies want. Yes, I do keep up on the news. I just want my family to be safe. The Chief and the guys in Ottawa can work this out with their country club buddies and leave my family the fuck alone."

Ella said, "You said fuck!"

Indy smiled without looking up.

Lane said, "Arthur said something about situations like this one." He felt their eyes turn to him. Even Indy lifted his head. "He told me that people like you and me," he pointed at Lori, Christine, Lauren and Dan. "Get the job done. Arthur said, `Let all those people at the top have all their little networking clubs, while the rest of us roll up our sleeves and get the job done.'"

"Arthur never said that!" Christine said.

"Yes, he did Mom," Indy said. "I heard him say it."

Lane lifted his chin. "I have a non-negotiable condition. You will cover childcare for Indy, Ella and Karen and protection for my family. Christine, Dan and Matt all work. I've been helping out with the kids." He made a circular motion with his hand "While I'm away this will all be taken care of."

Lori nodded. "I'll make it happen."

Christine stood, eyes wide, facing Lauren. "Where exactly are you taking him in Mexico?"

Lori said, "That's need-to-know for Lane and Lauren's safety."

When Lauren took the time to think about the intensity in Christine's voice, she realized she should have known what was coming.

Brenda stepped out of the shower. Experience taught her to allow time to think before sending any messages when she was feeling stressed. Fifteen to 20 minutes proved optimum.

She dried her hair. Her mind was clear and she'd edited a version of the text. She picked up the burner phone and tapped a text to Colin Wright.

We have a player in the game called 45. It is imperative that you alter established routines and alert personal security. I am doing the same. Further developments will be communicated as information becomes available.

45

CHAPTER 5

Lauren sat looking out the windows of the Calgary International Airport terminal where glass reached for the sky. The morning sun stretched shadows beyond the tails and wings of passenger aircraft waiting at the ends of the tunnels. Beyond the aircraft, the Rockies were snow tipped and magnified. This place had captured her. She could be anonymous here. A prairie girl starting fresh. This morning she wore grey yoga pants and a white tank top, choosing comfort for the four hour flight to San Jose, Cabos.

Her phone rang. She lifted her carry-on bag upright, unzipping the side, pulling out her phone.

What now? "Jackson."

"It's Christine, Paul Lane's niece. I got Lori to give me your number."

"Okay." Lauren leaned forward, ready to stand on the balls of her feet if necessary.

"We just dropped him off. He hasn't cleared security yet. I want to explain why I came on so strong. Why I'm so protective of my uncle."

"Go ahead." Lauren watched an SUV driving across the tarmac behind a pair of WestJet planes.

"You ever heard of Paradise in southern Alberta?"

"The polygamist community?" She turned as a guy in a muscle shirt walked past towing carry-on luggage.

"I escaped from there when I was sixteen. Uncle Lane and Uncle Arthur took me in. They looked out for me when no one else would. I got an education because of them. They are my family. My biological family is totally fucked up."

How can I explain I'm not a threat to you? "So are some of mine."

"Did the bishop from your church put you on his fuck chart while your mother did nothing to protect you?"

That is a new one. "No, but when a couple of guys from school grabbed me, turned me upside down to check and see what was under my skirt, I broke one guy's nose and the other's arm. Half the town and some of my extended family turned against me." *I couldn't go anywhere without people watching me, talking behind their hands.*

"How did you get out of that?"

Lauren looked around to see if anyone nearby was listening.

Tell her. Be upfront. "I put my head down, got a scholarship to the U of C."

"I came to Calgary with a garbage bag and the clothes on my back. One uncle turned me away. Lane and Arthur didn't."

"I haven't met Arthur."

Christine inhaled. "He died of a heart attack. Uncle Paul has been fighting depression ever since. He was just getting better. The job beat him up pretty good. He recovered after being shot. Then Arthur died. They were a team. A matched set. Arthur made Paul feel safe. He's lost."

"Okay?"

"What happened after you beat up those guys?"

What? No flies on her. Lauren sat up, focusing on the tip of one mountain peak. "The RCMP locked me up. They were going to charge me with assault. The boys came from wealthy families and they were hockey heroes."

"And then?"

"My mother found out what was happening. Got the story out of me. She went after Sergeant Bully."

"Sergeant Bully?"

"That's what we called him. He was the head of the RCMP in town. She took him on."

"How?"

"She knew about some of the shadier things Bully had been up to. Made some calls. Raised some hell about it. I was released. Bully retired. Mom and I were ostracized by the people in town who were chummy with Bully and the hockey heroes."

"So, you do know."

Lauren watched an airliner lift off, its wheels retracting into its belly. "What?"

"You know why I love my uncle. Why I'm so protective. Your Mom saved you. Uncle Lane saved me."

"Okay."

Christine paused. "I want you to take care of him. Watch out for him like your Mom looked out for you."

"I don't even know the guy."

"You will." Another pause. "They told you about the RPG right?"

"RPG?" *What the hell did I get myself into?*

"Ask him about the RPG. He has this knack for pissing powerful people off. I expect you to bring him home safe. Despite his talent for making enemies, and getting into trouble." Christine hung up.

Lauren stared at her phone, looking up. A woman passed in front of her followed by two teenage sons, thumbs texting, the father following with two rolling bags and two backpacks.

"Mind if I join you?"

She looked left. Lane stood in front of her wearing a long-sleeved light blue shirt, black shorts, sandals and a blue carry-on over his shoulder. She sat up, moving her bag to the floor. "Sure."

Lane sat down, looking around. Stood up and said, "You want a coffee?"

"Chai latte?" She reached into her bag for cash.

"My treat." Lane walked away.

Lauren's phone chirped. She looked at a text message from her mother.

Expecting you home for Kate's wedding.

She inhaled slowly, exhaling, counting down, using yogic breathing to suppress anxiety.

When Lane returned, she was breathing, air whistling through her nose, eyes closed, feet tucked underneath her, hands on knees, index fingers touching thumbs. He sipped his mocha with one hand, placing the chai under her nose with the other. Her right eyelid opened, and she took the cup. "Thanks."

Lane moved his bag next to hers and sat down, sipping coffee, taking in the mountains.

Lauren said, "I have to warn you."

"About what?"

"About this case and the people we're dealing with."

FRESALEAKS
Creating a more just society in the Americas
The Untouchables Are
Vulnerable and Dangerous

By V

MARTINA Villanova died of a gunshot to the head. Executed because she knew too much about the Untouchables.

The Untouchables (sometimes referred to as 45s or Oligarquía) remain loyal to the policies and practices of the 45th President of the United States. A recent series of scandals have created an environment where some of the 45s are feeling vulnerable.

In Canada they have been exposed for their connections to the Prime Minister's Office, resulting in the last government's defeat. In the United States the rejection of the policies of the 45th President have resulted in tougher rules and regulations as well as policies aimed at a more equitable distribution of that country's wealth. Mexican billionaires have begun to feel similar pressures.

In North America there appears to be a willingness to charge people and corporations who were at one time considered untouchable. This new political and social climate has made some of the Untouchables nervous as they struggle to expand their fortunes and status.

One of the ways the Untouchables have reacted is the arming and support of what some are calling a domestic terrorist wing of the 45s. It appears the 45s are behind the execution of Villanova, and the attempted murder of a Canadian who worked with her to expose illegal offshore accounts.

Lane was sandwiched between Lauren and the mother of teen boys sitting across the aisle, next to their father.

Mom wore white, Dad blue and the boys grey and green respectively. The boys were plugged into video games, while cheering, sometimes swearing and frequently arguing. The Dad had his headphones on while mom sporadically poked his arm, telling him, "Get them to stop."

Lauren popped another pink pill to stave off airsickness.

Mom leaned across Lane.

"Excuse me. I'm Andrea." She shook hands with Lauren. "Are those pills for airsickness?"

Lauren nodded, "I'm a nervous flier."

"Those pills are powerful. Be careful or you'll be in trouble after we land. How many have you taken?"

"Four."

"Four!?"

Lauren nodded.

Andrea leaned back, looking at Lane. "You might need a wheelchair after we land. Those antiemetics can really knock you on your ass."

Lane lifted his eyebrows, looking at Lauren who had stopped talking after a solid two hours of nervous chatter about how she'd learned Spanish in high school, then university. He'd learned all about her family in Saskatchewan and how she hadn't been back since an incident involving a "Sergeant Bully."

Lauren spent more than half an hour after that explaining why she felt so guilty for not going back to see her mother and told several stories designed to reveal her mother's strengths and her father's absence.

Ten minutes after Andrea's warning, Lauren's head leaned against the window. Her mouth was open and she snored.

Lane pulled his laptop out, plugged it in, putting on headphones, scrolling through the onboard movies three times. Finding nothing interesting, he opened the music on the laptop, closing his eyes and leaning his head back.

An hour later he felt the engines throttle back, initiating the descent. He looked right. Lauren's mouth was still open and her eyes closed. Out the window he could see the greens and deeper blues of the Sea of Cortez.

Andrea ignored her sons as they played tug of war with a tablet. She tapped Lane on the arm.

"Does she need a doctor? Want me to call the flight attendant?"

Lauren opened one eye. "I'm right here. I'm fine."

"But you are slurring your words." Andrea pointed a finger.

"Asshole!" One son yelled at the other.

Without turning, Andrea said, "You want me to come over

there?"

Lane thought, *They're almost within arm's length. Do something Andrea!* He leaned forward, spotting dad with his head tilted back, headphones on, eyes shut.

"Shithead," the other son said.

Arthur would have something to say. He turned to Andrea, making eye contact, asking, "How about you look after your boys? I'll look after my friend."

The stunned silence was followed by more prolonged quiet after she glared at her sons.

Ten minutes after landing, Lauren had a death grip on Lane's bicep. He carried both their bags as they weaved back and forth in a line approaching customs. Lauren walked with a Tower of Pisa tilt and would have fallen without his support. The customs official at the booth appeared unconcerned when Lane handed two passports over. The official stamped them, tucking the customs cards inside before waving them through.

Outside, Lauren held onto the handle of her pink rolling luggage, Lane dragged her along as she listed at a 15 degree angle. They passed a line of people holding signs for various resorts. Offloaded passengers began to huddle around resort reps while others headed for the bar with its faux beach bamboo veneer.

"Señor Lane?"

He turned to a round-faced woman with a Mayan nose and black hair tied into a bun. She wore a green T-shirt and khaki pants, smiled with perfect teeth, using her right hand to indicate they should follow. "Sígueme."

"No." Lane shook his head.

Lauren sounded as if she'd finished her eleventh margarita. "¿Cómo te llamas?"

"Angela." She waited, black irises impassive, chin lifted, arms at her sides.

Military, Lane thought.

Angela leaned in close, her voice low, head leaning to the left. "Andreas está a la espera."

Lauren gripped Lane's hand, rolling her luggage to follow Angela.

Lane followed. *Angela has warrior eyes.*

She led them to a silver Suburban. Lane spotted the driver looking over his shoulder, smiling. He recognized Andreas. His black hair was trimmed short on the sides, longer and styled on top, accented by a meticulously groomed beard. His wore white. At that moment, Lane sensed his old friend was no longer officially in the military.

Angela took Lauren by the elbow, guiding her to the rear seat.

Another woman appeared; her features sharper, more defined. She had her hair tied back in a bun, wearing a white T-shirt and khaki pants, opening the rear hatch of the Suburban, setting their bags inside. The woman indicated Lane should follow, guiding him to the front passenger side door, opening it for him.

Andreas asked, "How are you my friend?"

Lane closed the door, shaking hands. "I'm good." He looked over his shoulder at Lauren who blinked, closing her eyes for three seconds, opening her eyes, intent on focusing. He spotted Angela, her back to the Suburban, scanning the surroundings before climbing into the rear seat. Both women continued scanning outside the vehicle. Lane saw the second woman pull a handgun from the pocket at the back of the driver's seat, aiming it at the floor. He reached back, offering her his right hand. He noted the way she shifted the handgun to her left without taking her eyes off the outside.

"Lane."

"Petra." Her grip was firm with a quick release.

Andreas eased away from the curb. "Your friend is okay?" He glanced in Lauren's direction. She focused on a distant point.

"Her name is Lauren Jackson. She doesn't like flying."

Five minutes later, Lauren's head leaned against the doorframe, mouth open as she snored.

Forty minutes after that, the highway allowed a view of the Pacific. Lane spotted the telltale white spray of whales. He counted ten before the pod was hidden by a hill. Thirty minutes later the desert was replaced with farms and palm trees.

Andreas said, "After we get everyone settled, I know a coffee shop you will like."

Soon they were parked inside the grey cinder brick walls of an oasis of palm trees, multicoloured bougainvillea, sand covered pathways and the adobe walls of a pink bungalow fronting a cobblestone driveway.

A third woman in khaki pants and red T-shirt observed their arrival, one hand resting on the handgun on her hip, her shoulder leaning on a veranda pillar. She was taller, willowy.

Lane helped Lauren as they followed Petra, who toted their luggage over the patio, rolling it click-clacking down a tiled hallway to two bedrooms whose doors faced one another. She lifted her hand off one suitcase, opening the door, pointing at Lauren.

Lane helped Lauren through the door. She made for the white topped comforter, sitting down, leaning left till her head hit the pillow, allowing Lane to take her shoes off.

He closed her door, walked across the hall, then rolled his luggage into one corner while Petra retreated up the hallway.

The room had a six foot square, North-facing window, with a vibrant red bougainvillea blooming within arm's length. The walls were white with a wardrobe of solid wood. On the other wall was a mirror and dresser made of the same heavy ebony.

Lane lifted his bag onto the bed and unzipped it, hanging his shirts in the wardrobe. It smelled of eucalyptus oil.

There was a knock on the door. He turned to see Andreas, arms crossed, white shirt, shorts and sandals.

"Would you like a short walk and a coffee?"

"How long have you been out of the army?" Lane hung up the last shirt.

"Three years." Andreas shrugged.

"Where is the general?" Lane smiled. "Tu abuelo."

"He plans to be here tomorrow in the morning." Andreas looked over his shoulder. "Lauren is your bodyguard?"

"She has been the lead on the investigation. She speaks Spanish and is a police officer." Lane lowered his voice, waving two fingers and a thumb. "Your tres chicas?"

"Adelitas." Andreas pointed a finger back. "How do you say feroz?"

"Ferocious?"

He nodded, "They did some sensitive work combating the cartels." He looked around. "Could we leave for the café now? Todos Santos closes down around five."

Lane followed Andreas along the hallway, into the spacious living room, outside onto the covered patio with its table and eight chairs. They followed the cobblestone driveway, through the door set into the wall to one side of the locked front gate guarded by Petra. She nodded as they passed.

Andreas said, "Cafelix."

Petra lifted her chin, locking the door behind them as they stepped out onto a cobblestone road angling its way up to the centre of town. Multicoloured banners hung over the roadway. Most of the two-storied buildings had half-finished walls spiked with rebar. Palm trees formed a backdrop to most structures.

"Thank you," Lane said.

Andreas waited while leading the way uphill.

"I mean gracias for getting us here." Lane looked left as a black SUV passed. It had a pair of speakers secured to its roof rack with bungee cords. There was a blast of mariachi interspersed with Spanish. "Spaying and neutering is free here?"

"Yes, the good doctor is trying to manage our dog and cat populations. You have been practicing your Spanish."

Lane nodded as they reached the intersection to the town's main street where shops, cafés and the red-walled Hotel California enticed tourists. "It keeps my mind busy. I understand most of what I hear. My vocabulary and conversation need a lot of work."

He looked left then right, catching a glimpse of a red T-shirted adelita about 100 metres behind them. "What is her name?"

Andreas looked over his shoulder. "Maria."

"Adelita?" Lane followed Andreas to the right as he walked onto the patio of a coffee shop where a sculpted skeleton sat on a wicker chair with a round 'Cafélix' sign resting against its ribs.

"We have a tradition of women warriors. My amigos worked together in that capacity against the cartels. They are very good."

"Lethal?"

Andreas looked directly at Lane, nodding, "If necessary," before leading the way inside where he ordered coffees from the short-haired woman behind the counter who wore a white apron and T-shirt. They went back outside, sitting in red chairs behind the half wall separating them from the street.

Lane looked around at the empty tables. "Can we talk here?"

Andreas nodded. "The owner is one of ours. Her name is Gabriella."

Lane watched three dogs of diverse parentage run across the street. Thirty seconds later he could hear the vet and his speakers approaching. "It looks like the dogs know what the vet is up to."

The café owner brought their coffees, leaving with a nod to Andreas.

Lane sipped his mochaccino, smiled and asked, "I've read the reports on the death of Villanova in Mexico City and the attack on Singer in Calgary. I've also seen the notes from the Singer interviews and the background on WTF and CNIG. The problem is I'm really not clear on why I'm needed here."

"My abuelo trusts you and we have some information implicating very powerful people in your country, mine..." he pointed at his chest, "and the United States."

"You mean the 45s? The information on them is sketchy at

best."

Andreas held his hands up and apart. "Bigger than them."

Lane set his coffee down. "How big?"

"Enorme." Andreas looked across the street at a lone palm tree backlit by the sun. "Some of us call it la oligarquía, others call it the church; the super-rich who worship money above all things."

"You and your abuelo have a plan?"

Andreas lifted his chin as the woman behind the counter said, "Mas?" He looked at Lane who drained his cup, then nodded.

Andreas held up two fingers. "Dos, por favor."

He looked back at Lane. "The general knew Mexico needed expanded intelligence operations especially with all that talk of a wall. I remember him phoning me one night explaining how he had seen a show about icebergs. It gave him an idea. He's been working on it for the last few years.

"Many Latinos work for the super wealthy. We are gardeners, waitresses, housekeepers, janitors, workers of all sorts–the underwater icebergs if you like. He knew the rich tended to act as if we did not exist, that we could not speak the language, or forgot we were there. The general has established a network of intelligence agents who gathered a remarkable library of information. The tragic killing of Señora Villanova and a combination of other events has led us to believe the time to act is upon us."

"What kind of action, exactly?"

"Surgery with a big hammer."

Lane opened his mouth, thought better of it, looking over the roof of the brick building across as the sun settled into long shadow. He felt a glimmer of expectation thrumming his ribs, closing his eyes, smiling.

Brenda wore her pink Queen's University onesie with white trim on the pockets. She sipped chamomile tea, waiting for KG to pick up. KG was short for Kush Gumbay-Yaw and those who knew of him inevitably warned her to address him with the acronym.

Brenda glanced at the oven clock, verifying it was exactly 7 pm KG time – or Mountain Standard Time as most people knew it. He lived somewhere in the western US and had responded to her text with an exact time for contact.

She dialed the number he'd provided. He answered on the fifth ring.

"KG? It's Brenda."

"Okay?" He had a deep radio voice, which sounded almost Canadian.

"I consult for some financial companies in Canada."

"I know."

"One of my employers died under unfortunate circumstances."

KG sniffed. "Really?"

Brenda heard the slight change in pitch. "Yes, his death is being investigated. I believe he may have made some threatening statements to some powerful investors."

"If that's all you have to say, I'm a very busy man."

"My concern is with the 45s and their uneasiness about what my former employer might or might not say. With my former employer's departure, there is renewed openness to the kinds of economic policies supported by the 45s. I wanted to get that message to them. Unfortunately, it appears I am operating under the misconception that you were the person to contact. I apologize for this intrusion."

Brenda hung up, returning to her tea.

CHAPTER 6

Lane woke up with Baja sun in his face. He rolled onto his back, looking at the sand coloured ceiling before checking his phone, seeing it was almost seven.

His mind and emotions were red raw from dreams of Arthur and having dinner together in Beirut, even though neither had ever been there. He recalled a promenade, palm trees, sand and the Mediterranean. They sat sipping after dinner coffee, tasting like it was computer generated. Arthur sitting across, wearing khaki shorts and white shirt, left knee over right, pixels showing.

Lane sat up, putting his feet on the cool of the tile floor, then stood, pulled on shorts, heading for the washroom where he could turn on the shower and try to wash away the dream.

Coffee's aromatic DNA made him close his eyes and inhale as he opened the door to his room, wearing fresh clothes.

He followed its genetic code along the hallway into the kitchen with its green, red and blue backsplash, red tiled floor and cypress cabinets. The sliding glass doors opened to a veranda where potted plants and bougainvillea painted a Matisse. Petra and Angela switched from Spanish to English as he entered.

Angela pointed at the carafe on the counter, switching back

to Spanish, "Sevir café," turning to Petra, "You economists, always get confused by the numbers. The numbers are people; living, breathing entities. Not numbers on a spreadsheet."

Lane opened the cabinet above the carafe, then another, searching for a mug.

Petra said, "You miss the point. The economy and the capital are necessary for supporting schools and hospitals in a modern society. The people and the numbers are interconnected." She took a few steps, opening a cupboard for Lane. "Just because you are a doctor does not mean you are an expert in other fields."

"I am missing nothing. You are forgetting that we are flesh and blood."

Lane stirred milk into his coffee before stepping through the open glass door, onto the patio.

Andreas sat watching a hummingbird zip from one flower to the next. He turned as Lane sat down, then said, "It is quieter out here. They are always discussing politics, economics and social science. I prefer watching the hummingbirds."

Lane held his breath as the hummingbird hovered about two meters away.

"Where is Maria?"

Andreas smiled. "Outside on guard. On those rare occasions when the three of them debate, there is even more passion. She is a cyber specialist who knows human nature better than the others. They are all well-educated and very intelligent."

"And lethal." Lane watched for Andreas' reaction.

He looked sideways at Lane. "If necessary."

This is as good a time as any. "When are you going to tell me the real reason why I'm here?"

Lauren opened one eye, taking in the pink adobe wall a few

centimetres from her nose, rolling over, wiping the drool from her cheek, realizing she was wearing the clothing from the morning before. She squeezed her eyes shut, sitting up, heading out to find a place to pee.

Thirty minutes later, she walked into the kitchen, red-faced, feeling the scrutiny of the women at the table. One stood, opening a cabinet door, pouring a coffee, handing it to Lauren who said, "Gracias." She sat across from the two women.

"Me llamo Lauren."

"We know." The woman in the green T-shirt pointed at the one in black, "Petra," then at herself, "Angela." The women sized her up with frank curiosity.

Petra asked, "Feeling better?"

"Much, thank you." She eyed the bananas in the bowl at the centre of the table.

Angela slid the bowl closer to Lauren, "There are some enchiladas in the fridge."

"Oh yes please, por favor, I'm starving." Lauren peeled a banana as she stood, turning, heading for the fridge.

As she opened the door, she heard Angela say, "Aquí nos encontramos con dos chicos que nacen con pollas en sus bocas."

Lauren turned. "Is that a fucking problem for you?"

Angela smiled, standing, reaching into a drawer near the sink, pulling out a Glock in a holster, setting it on the counter next to the fridge. "Not a problem for me. An observation. You know how to use this?"

She winked at Lauren before turning and walking outside.

She was playing you. Lauren shut the fridge door, the gun under her arm, coffee in her right. She went out onto the patio. "What's up?"

Brenda recognized the number displayed on the screen in her

SUV. She waited behind a panel van in rush hour traffic on Crowchild Trail where it crossed over the Bow River. She pressed the green button on the screen. "Brenda here."

"You interested in an exchange of information?"

She looked right, seeing a man up to the knuckle in his nose. "What kind of information KG?"

"Some people need to know who is looking into a certain event in Mexico City and a similar occurrence in your area. My friends want to know names and locations."

"In exchange for?"

"Information to help you with the problem related to your late employer."

"I'll see what I can come up with." She reached over, pressing end as traffic began to move.

Hashir got the first look from a surveillance camera inside 'Isham's Donair," a daughter and father eatery across the street from Wright's office tower.

It was his second twelve hour day in front of the monitor, checking images obtained from the street approaching the tower.

The suspect wore black pants, jacket and toque, hands in his pockets as he jaywalked across 6th Avenue. He headed for the underground parking, ducking under the yellow and black barrier less than 30 minutes before Wright's estimated time of death.

Hashir's cell chirped. He froze the image on his computer, glancing at his phone, seeing his daughter, arms raised after scoring a goal at her soccer game. He stood up, fists in the air.

"My Zena scored a goal!"

A message from Rhonda appeared in the corner of his screen. "Send me the pic. I wanna see."

He forwarded the image from his wife, then went back to

work, thinking about 6th Avenue and the fact it was a one-way heading west.

He calculated the most likely route the killer would take to the airport.

Lauren was there when Maria shouldered her Xiuhcoatl assault rifle before opening the front gate admitting a '70s Chev pickup. Its hood was faded black, red stripes running along its white flanks. Lauren noticed the pickup's engine throbbed happily at idle and the tires were new. Maria checked both ways down the street before closing the gate.

The pickup eased in, parking next to the Suburban. The driver wore a black Stetson, stained salty white where crown and brim met. His long-sleeved shirt was white like his hair and his blue jeans were faded the same shade in places.

He reached behind the cab, lifting a leather duffle bag out, hugging Maria with one arm before heading for the front door. As he reached it, Andreas opened the door, stepping out, hugging the man around the neck.

"Hey, Lori? It's Christine. You know, Lane's niece." She sat in her kitchen, feet up on a chair, watching her kids. Ella sat on the couch, watching 'The Parent Trap' on her iPod. Indy was curled up on the easy chair creating a park for dinosaurs on his iPod.

Karen, the newborn, was cocooned in a blanket, tucked in the crook of Christine's left arm. Alexandra slept upstairs after feeding Karen.

Lori said, "Good hearing from you. Again, sorry about Arthur. I wanted to talk with you at the funeral but never got the chance."

She's trying to steer me away from Lane. Christine looked out the window at the trees with their first ripe green leaves. "I think we were all numb. One day we were all together, then the heart attack happened. Thanks for the quilts by the way. The kids love them."

"Happy to do it. The help working out?"

Christine looked to Rory sitting on the other end of the couch next to Ella. The officer wore her blues, had her red hair tied back, constantly checking her phone for texts from the regular patrols passing outside. She kept getting up to take a look out the windows.

"The kids like Rory. I just wish she would relax a bit."

"How's the new babe?"

Christine looked at Karen's face, her black curly hair and ultra-soft eyelids. "She's perfect."

"I'd love to see some pictures."

"I want to know how my uncle is doing and I need to know where he is."

"You know I can't talk about that, especially over the phone."

Especially?

"Sorry, gotta go. Couple of my quilter friends are coming over tonight to drink a little wine. Take care of yourself and that family of yours." Lori hung up.

Christine put her feet on the floor, standing up, flipping through the contacts on her phone, finding one, pressing 'call.' "Hey Anna, it's Christine. I need a favour."

Lane sat at the kitchen table. Angela appeared with the red and white first aid kit, which was more like a suitcase. She opened it, removing a sterile dressing, handing him a piece of gauze. He rolled it, opening his fist, pressing the dressing onto his palm, gripping it tight. She handed him a wipe. He cleaned up the blood on the table. She set a blue pad under his hand.

Angela held her palm out. "I need your index finger."

He complied and she jabbed the end of the finger with a needle. "Ouch."

"Good. No nerve damage." She opened his palm, surveying the wound, its open lips still bleeding. "Stitches won't work there." She closed his fist, turning to search through the bag.

"What did you do to him?" Lauren asked as she walked into the kitchen with a bowl of fresh veggies from the garden.

Lane shook his head. "I was cutting a cucumber and missed."

"Clumsy." Angela held up a plastic vial of purple liquid. "First I will irrigate the wound, then glue it shut."

Lauren set the vegetables on the counter before coming closer to watch Angela work.

Lane yawned.

Angela frowned. "It doesn't hurt?"

"I don't know why I did that."

Lauren asked, "Did what?"

Lane said, "Yawned and yes it does hurt."

Angela opened Lane's hand, squirting a saline solution into the wound.

Lane winced.

Angela wiped the blood away with gauze before applying the purple glue. "You will have to keep it dry for the next 24 hours." She looked at Lauren. "You can help me prepare lunch?"

Ella led the way on her scooter, Christine pushing the stroller with sleeping Karen wrapped in a blanket. Indy followed. Christine had her uncle's laptop tucked underneath the baby as they walked home in the warm spring air.

The computer had been sitting on the counter of his condo

when they arrived. She'd recharge it when they got home.

Lane pulled the legs, head and shell away from the shrimp before popping the flesh into his mouth. He wore a white surgical glove on his left hand, keeping the wound dry and clean.

Angela sat across the table deftly dismembering shrimp and popping them in her mouth. Former General Rodriguez, now Minister of Justice, sat at one head of the table and Maria at the other. Petra was outside with Lauren on sentry duty.

Rodriguez wiped his fingers with a red napkin, reaching for a sip of beer from a long-necked bottle. He set the bottle down. "It is time to discuss what we know, what we need to know and what we plan to do."

Lane asked, "What about Lauren and Petra?"

Rodriguez raised his chin. "My daughter is briefing your Lauren as we speak."

Petra is your aunt. Lane looked at Andreas who was staring back at him.

Andreas smiled, leaning his head to one side.

Rodriguez said, "We have been in close contact with CSIS, in particular with Keely Saliba for more than a year about an issue of interest to both our countries. Many of our wealthiest have been avoiding paying their taxes by hiding their fortunes in banks around the world. Within a week we plan to have those monies placed in a new bank." He nodded at Maria.

She chewed and swallowed a wedge of tomato before sipping water. "We have set a up a virtual bank called 'V Bank' operating in Mexico and Canada. We also plan to create a U.S. branch in the event the first stage of our operation succeeds."

Angela said, "The money in V Bank will be used to offer loans for hospitals, public schools, water purification and deserving individuals. In the case of hospitals, preference will be given to applications supporting patient care. School loans will be focused on students and their needs."

Andreas set his water down. "The initial recovery will be coordinated from here and by the people in this room working with our operatives in Mexico, Canada, the U.S. and other countries where tax havens exist."

Rodriguez lifted his chin at Lane. "You and Señorita Jackson will monitor any actions jeopardizing our operation. We believe the murder in Mexico City and the attempted murder in Calgary are evidence of this threat. We must assume it is real and be prepared to counter it. Your job will be to keep us ahead of that threat."

Andreas said, "Our intelligence indicates a U.S. based group called the 45s is behind the killing."

Maria pushed her hair behind her ears. "There is one other problem." She pointed at Lane.

What's this?

"Your brother."

"Joseph? What's he got to do with this?"

Maria's eyebrows lifted. "Joseph Lane is one of the clients of the banks we are infiltrating. His assets will be affected."

Lane thought, *My brother never called, never showed up for Arthur's funeral.* Joseph's complete disregard for Arthur reignited Lane's rage. "Let's get started."

There were few things Christine hated more than being late. She was late getting the kids to bed. Dan was late getting home from work. Matt was late taking Alexandra and Karen home. A worse thing was being stuck in the mental muck of a dilemma. She was fiercely protective of Lane, her children and Dan, her sister, Matt and now Karen.

Christine knew it was unfair to blame Lori for her state of mind but that would have been lying.

She parked across the street from Lori's pink, stucco bungalow with its garage around back and a black Cadillac SUV parked out front. Behind the SUV was a white Land Rover.

Christine didn't think about the implications of the luxury SUVs and didn't look either way as she crossed the street, hurrying up the front walk, poking the doorbell with her middle finger. She ignored the internal warning advising her to take a breath and think before opening her mouth.

Lori opened the front door, her blonde hair loose on her shoulders. She studied Christine without smiling, another early warning Christine ignored. "I need to know where my uncle is."

Lori stood back, holding the door open. "Come in. There's plenty of wine." She turned, heading down the hallway. "We're in the dining room."

Christine took off her running shoes, catching a glimpse of her dark eyes in the wall mirror, her black, unruly hair matching her state of mind. Her heels pounded the hardwood floor, then she stood in the doorway to the dining room.

The table for eight was covered with a blue, pink, silver and scarlet quilt. The women looked back at her, holding glasses of wine.

The woman with the short grey hair Christine recognized immediately as Joy Wasnicky, the chair of the school board and technically her boss. The third woman had jet-black hair. It was Councillor Stephanie Ware, whose complexion was a shade darker than Christine's. It was rumoured Ware was about to run for mayor.

Lori handed Christine a glass of wine. "This is Christine Lane, a friend of mine." She pointed at Christine's glass. "Take a sip and sit." She indicated an empty chair next to hers.

Christine sat, staring at the glass of wine before lifting it to her lips and draining the red. She lifted her eyes to meet Lori's. "My uncle needs me. I'm going to wherever he is as soon as I find out exactly where that is."

Lori refilled Christine's glass.

"Anna wouldn't tell me where. She says it's too risky for him and for me." Christine drained the second glass. "I'm asking for your help."

Lori topped up Christine's glass before smiling at Joy and Stephanie. "I know you're worried and I am too. I just can't tell you what you want to know."

Christine looked at the wine, its legs running down the glass. "Since Arthur died, Uncle Paul's been fading, losing weight, losing interest in life. We hoped moving him into a new place would help but it didn't." She ran her thumb up and down the glass. "He told me he always felt safe with Arthur around. Not many people knew Arthur was Paul's protector. That's just the way it was with them. We all knew that. Now my Uncle Paul has lost his protector."

She looked at Lori, feeling the wine going to her head, losing her focus. "I need to go there. To be with him. To let my Uncle Paul know that Arthur isn't the only one he can count on."

Lori leaned closer. "I know your uncle. He knows he can count on you. I can't tell you where he is because it would put him in danger."

"You don't understand."

Lori shook her head.

"Lane and Arthur stepped up for me and Matt when we had nowhere to go. Now he needs one of us to step up. Matt gets it. I get it." She shrugged, taking in the watchful expressions from the women in the room.

"That's what matters." Christine touched her sternum. "To me."

CHAPTER 7

Christine woke with the pink and orange sunrise filling their living room window. She looked at the blue and gold quilt covering her as she lay on the couch. *Shit!* Memories of drunken ramblings while being driven home by Joy.

Footsteps on the stairs – Indy in his blue soccer shirt and pajama bottoms came to her, lifting the quilt, snuggling up beside. "Where did you get this blanket Mom?"

The scent of her son's hair prompted a flashback of Lane standing up to her mother and the men she'd brought from Paradise. Christine's mother Alison had been intent on kidnapping Indy from Neonatal Intensive Care at the Foothills Medical Centre. Christine recalled Lane's calm voice, standing his ground, protecting newborn Indy and Christine until hospital security arrived.

She squeezed Indy closer and he sighed. Even Dan's mother Lola had stood firm, protecting Indy. The only unselfish act Lola had managed so far.

He said, "Look at the window Mom. It's beautiful."

She looked out to an orange sky. An old wave of guilt washed over Christine when she remembered how she'd listened to the people at Paradise who talked about her uncles' lifestyle. How Lane and Arthur had been her second choice when she escaped the compound. The way her uncles took her in, not judging, just listening and loving. It had taken a year to come to understand the significance of living in a home without judgment.

Brenda drank tea: a special blend of Tieguanyin steeped for three minutes and 25 seconds. She took her first sip, closing her eyes, taking a second before reaching for her burner phone.

It had been relatively easy to get the detective's name. It took one call to the office of Barrett Duval, alderman and vice-chair of the police commission. He had made it known he wished to be considered for the party nomination when the next federal by-election came up. A hint to Barrett that the name of an officer on special assignment would move him to the top of the nomination list and Brenda had what she needed.

She sipped as she dialed. It rang four times, then an electronic voice said, "Leave a message."

Brenda looked at the pearls on the edges of the tea in the china cup. She'd never met this contact known as Willcocks but had come to rely on the operative. Brenda knew the data would be accurate after seven years of using Willcocks to supply information when she needed it to put out a fire for the PMO.

She left a voice message. "I need information on the whereabouts of Lauren Jackson, homicide detective with CPS. The usual incentives are in play. If your investigation leads to an accurate location, there will be a bonus of $10,000." She hung up.

Lori picked up the call an hour later. "Office of the Chief Constable."

"It's Rhonda. We may have a problem. I just found out about a call that came in about 30 minutes ago – someone from the police commission inquiring if we had any detectives on special assignment. A rookie took the call and disclosed Lauren's name."

Lori said, "Shit!"

Rhonda inhaled.

"Sorry. Can you backtrack the call and determine its source?"

"Nigel, Hashir, and I are already on it."

Lori tucked the phone next to her ear and began typing. "As soon as you have a name, I want to know. And no more leaks. The people we are dealing with are ruthless. Understood?"

"Of course. Why do you think I called?"

Lauren said, "It's kind of creepy, that's all."

They sat having coffee at 'Cafélix.' The skeletal sculpture sat near the doorway.

"Something about death being democratic." Lane looked at the skeleton, then across the street. "I wonder if we could take a walk around town."

"I know what it means. I'm just sayin' it's creepy." She crossed her ankles.

Lane pulled the phone from the pocket of his blue shirt, reading a text from Christine. "My niece wants to know how we are and where we are." He tapped out "I'm good," added a smiley face imoji with sunglasses and sent the message.

Lauren looked out on the street as two dogs ran past. "Looks like the vet is back."

He smiled, reaching for his coffee as the mariachi music opened up from the loudspeakers on the roof of the vet's car.

Her phone chirped. She reached for it, reading the message. "My brother wants to know if I'm going to be his date for my sister's wedding."

"Are you?"

She shrugged while replying with a rainbow emoji.

Lane lifted his eyebrows. "Why a rainbow?"

She set the phone down, looked at him for a moment. "My brother is gay. When he was sixteen, he climbed the water tower in town. My mother and I had to climb up there and talk him down. The same people who harassed him for being gay said he was so useless he couldn't get suicide right. I'd already decided to get away from home. I got a scholarship to the U of C. My brother moved to Calgary with me and we haven't been back since."

"Now I understand."

"What exactly?"

Lane smiled. "Why you got angry with Angela."

Lauren opened her mouth.

Lane held up a hand. "Please let me finish. I asked Andreas about Angela saying we were born with dicks in our mouths. He said he trusts his life to these women. He called what Angela said a joke between friends. If anyone outside their circle said it to Andreas or to me, there would be trouble and Angela would be the first to step up."

Lauren shook her head.

"I understand something else."

Lauren took a long exhale.

"What's that?"

"Why you don't like to fly."

She nodded. "Ever since the water tower, I get flashbacks." She reached for her coffee. "What about you? What can you tell me about yourself?" She pointed at Lane's phone. "Why are Nigel, Lori and your niece so protective of you?"

Lane shrugged.

Lauren waited.

"Rough year."

Lauren waited.

"My husband died in January. Heart attack. We'd only been

married a couple of years. We'd been together more than twenty-five."

"I'm sorry. I don't know what else to say."

Lane shrugged. "There isn't much to say. I've moved into a condo close to our… my niece's place. Matt and Alexandra just had a baby."

"Matt and Alexandra?"

"Arthur's nephew came to live with us, then he married Christine's sister Alexandra. Sounds incestuous I know." He hesitated. "It isn't."

Sensing Lane's discomfort, Lauren decided to change the subject. "How do you know Rodriguez and Andreas?"

He smiled. "They arrested Nigel and me at a wedding."

"Whose wedding?"

"Anna and Nigel's."

Lauren lifted her eyebrows. "And the rocket propelled grenade?"

Lane turned his head to one side, watching her with his left eye. "Who told you about that?"

She shrugged, smirking.

"That came later. By that time Rodriguez was starting to trust us."

Lauren nodded. "So that's why he trusts you and why he wanted you here?"

"That's part of it. He and I have similar outlooks. Similar values."

She drained her coffee. "Will you tell me about the RPG?"

"We were ambushed on a gravel road somewhere inland from Cancun. Andreas was shredding them with a heavy machine gun. A couple of bad guys made it to the edge of the jungle. One was carrying something that looked like a heavy weapon. I returned fire, wounded him and he missed his aim with the RPG."

Her phone chirped. She reached for it, reading the text. "We may have a problem. Someone back home is checking on our whereabouts."

Hashir pressed a key on his laptop, projecting an image on the screen. He was in the conference room with Nigel who sat to his left and Rhonda on his right.

Hashir waited for the passport photo to appear. The man had close cut blonde hair, an angelic, angular face and blue eyes. He was described as five feet eleven inches, weighing 180 pounds and thirty-two years of age.

"This is who I tracked from the Wright murder scene to airport security at Calgary International. The name on the passport is Donald Colton and his place of birth listed as Allentown, Pennsylvania. He was on a flight from Calgary to Las Vegas. That's all I have on him so far."

Nigel asked, "What about the call asking about Lauren's whereabouts?"

Hashir tapped a key, the second image appeared. It was a list of phone numbers and locations. "The call to our desk came from the office of Alderman Barrett Duvall."

Rhonda pointed at the screen. "And the outgoing calls from Duvall's office?"

"One cell phone number stands out. It was an incoming call to Duvall's office ten minutes prior to the call to us. The same number was called about fifteen minutes later from Duvall's office. As far as I can tell, the number is for a prepaid cellphone."

Nigel pointed at Rhonda. "We're going to need to get eyes and ears on Duvall." He pointed at Hashir. "Any way we can track the prepaid cell phone without tipping our hand?"

Hashir said, "I have another idea."

Nigel asked, "What is it?"

Hashir put a third image on the screen. "The prepaid cell phone number appears on a call from Colin Wright's office."

"Absofuckinlutely fantastic!" Nigel stood. "We can track

Colin Wright's calls as part of our investigation into his father's death."

Rhonda smacked the table with a manila folder. She pointed at Nigel. "Sit down. There's more. You asked me to check on the WTF board. I found something."

Nigel's face was red as he sat.

Rhonda looked from Nigel to Hashir who said, "Don't do that!"

"What?" Nigel asked.

Hashir kept his voice low and his eyes on Nigel. "Disrespect her by asking her to do a job, then not letting her have a say."

Nigel nodded, hand over his mouth, hiding a smile.

Rhonda opened the folder, passing each of the men a sheet of paper embossed with the WTF logo. "I checked the names. Look at the bottom, see Brenda Bruciarsi? She worked in the shadows of the PMO before the Cyprus Scandal. I think there might be one picture of her on Google. She dropped out of sight just before the scandal hit and resurfaced in Calgary. She's a fixer. We need to take a very close look at her."

Rhonda stabbed Bruciarsi's name with her forefinger. "I'd put money on her being the puppet-master."

Christine closed her eyes. The kids were asleep, Dan on his way home, Matt snoring on the couch. Rory was outside checking things out and Alexandra was feeding the baby. Christine opened her eyes, lifting her phone off the kitchen table, clicking a quick photo of Alexandra, her black hair tied back, face free of makeup, holding her daughter's hand.

Alexandra looked up. "What are you doing?"

Christine smiled. "You two look beautiful together."

"She is gorgeous, isn't she? I wish she would sleep more."

Christine stood, heading for the cupboard, getting water

for her sister.

Alex took the glass and a sip, setting it down. "Where is your uncle's laptop?"

"What for?" Christine crossed her arms.

Alexandra looked up.

Christine recognized her sister's expression.

She's got that 'nobody tells me what to do' look.

"Nobody knows your uncle better than us. We can figure out his password." She looked over her shoulder. "Hurry up. We have a few minutes to ourselves and Karen won't be blowing our cover – yet."

Willcock's text message came as Brenda opened the lasagna in the aluminum dish delivered from her favourite Calgary restaurant. She decided it wasn't up to Toronto standards, but it was getting there. She leaned over, licked tomato sauce from her thumb and forefinger, opening the text.

Subject was on a flight to San Jose, Cabos.
Arrived Sunday, May 7, accompanied by one Paul Lane.
Further details to follow.

Brenda considered the information as she used a spatula to move the lasagna from container to white plate. Then she reached for her phone, sending two texts.

She smiled when done, remembering how she had become adept at using phones and laptops to fix the most complex of problems, often without ever getting out of her pajamas.

KG perched with the driver's door open. His black Ram four-by-four, diesel powered, jacked-up pickup idled behind his 3,000 square foot, custom log home with a four car garage. Atop the garage were sleeping quarters for up to six of the men he called his soldiers.

He wore desert camouflage pants, cowboy boots, a green T-shirt and white Stetson. At six feet four inches, weighing 300 pounds, with dyed blond hair and blue eyes, he demanded attention. He looked down on Chris Spicer. "We may have a job coming up. I need you to get into the armoury."

"Which weapons were you thinking?" Chris was just under six feet tall, weighed 170 pounds and was black-haired. He wore green pants and a black 'SEAL Team 6' T-shirt.

"The HKs and M249s should do it. Get extra clips and some M67s. We'll be taking out some Mexicans, so it'll be light work."

Chris thought, *What's an M67? I'll have to check YouTube for operating the M249.* "No problem."

KG lifted his double chin in the direction of the vacuum truck sucking his septic tank dry. "Who's the Hosey with the honey wagon?"

Chris turned to look at the white three-ton truck with the black tank. A black-haired man in blue coveralls operated the vacuum hose inserted into the septic tank's access hatch. "Enrique. Doesn't speak any English. He won't be here much longer."

KG nodded as he closed his door, starting the diesel, shifting into drive, leaning an elbow out the open window. "Get the equipment loaded in the Expedition. I'll be back later."

Half an hour later, Enrique stopped at a rest stop on Highway 77, north of Tucson and Mount Lemmon. The mountain was dappled with sunshine and shadow under a cloudy sky. He reached for the phone on the passenger seat while the engine idled.

Andreas set his phone on the table, stood, looking around for his grandfather who liked to putter with the bougainvillea and snack on fresh strawberries. The sun was low in the sky, shadows were long, colours intense.

Lauren and Maria were on guard duty. Angela insisted on preparing supper and Petra sat at the dinner table with her laptop.

Andreas found Lane and his abuelo behind a magnificent scarlet bougainvillea. They were sitting in lawn chairs, eating fresh strawberries from a bowl on the ground between them. Andreas stopped when he heard their voices.

Rodriguez said, "I never knew my father. I was always studying other families, looking for an example I could follow. How did you learn to be a father?"

Lane laughed. "By doing the opposite of what my parents did."

"You haven't laughed in a very long time?"

"You could tell?"

"Si. Yes."

Lane popped a strawberry in his mouth, chewing, closing his eyes. "These things are like little bombs. The flavour explodes in your mouth."

"Why did you change the topic?"

Lane was silent.

Rodriguez said, "The soldiers I have fought beside are the ones I find it easiest to talk with. There are no, how you say? Mentiras?"

"We call it bullshit. The people you can be honest with. There is no bullshit between people like us. I think that is what you are trying to say."

"Then?"

"I killed a man. He was going to shoot a boy and kill the rest of his family. I shot him first. I kept seeing him in my dreams. I shot out one of his eyes. For years afterward there were nightmares."

Rodriguez settled, waiting.

"Then Arthur died. He had a heart attack, I found him on the couch, tried CPR, called an ambulance. Nothing worked.

Arthur and I..." He interlaced his fingers "We were close. He was fierce about protecting us, our family. Now he's gone." Lane shrugged.

"I remember Arthur. Fierce is a good word for him."

"I miss him."

"Grief is like the sea. It runs in waves. Every so often, a big one knocks us off our feet. We are helpless against it."

Lane nodded. The silence expanded. A green hummingbird whirred around the bougainvillea. Lane and Rodriguez turned, spotting Andreas.

Rodriguez asked, "What is it?"

"Lo siento. Sorry." Andreas held out his phone. "We have a message and some pictures of 45s. Our source says they are getting ready for an operation."

Rodriguez took the phone, flipping through the pictures before handing it to Lane. "What do you suggest we do now, mi amigo?"

Chris Spicer was relieved when he found two videos. One explained how to use an M67 grenade. He studied the other, showing him how to attach an M249 magazine, lift the cover and feed mechanism and operate the safety for the machine gun affectionately known as 'the SAW.'

Now I know what to call it. 'The SAW.'

He practiced loading, feeding, and cocking at least twenty times before packing two 'SAWS', four HK assault rifles, twenty M67 grenades and six Glock handguns away in the aluminum toolbox at the back of the Expedition.

Spicer sat down in the shade of the SUV's lift gate, pulled out a notebook and began writing a checklist. The sun was low in the western sky, promising some respite from the day's heat. He went over his list, adding items until the darkness sent him inside.

Rory had gone home, replaced by Constable Eric Manywounds. He was six feet tall, weighing maybe 190 pounds and loved to talk baseball with Matt. While they talked in the living room, Karen slept in the bassinet.

Christine and Alexandra crossed another password off the list. They were on their second sheet of loose leaf.

The couch sighed as Eric stood. "I should do a check outside."

Christine shivered, spotting the Glock on his hip.

Alexandra smiled at Eric. "Thanks for keeping us safe." She tried another password as Eric stepped out the front door. "Let's get ten more done before Karen wakes up."

CHAPTER 8

Christine woke up just after three that morning. Dan snored next to her. She listened for other sounds, hearing none, closing her eyes.

I wonder. She lifted the blankets, rolling out of bed, padding downstairs.

Eric sat in the easy chair, watching her, lifting his eyebrows.

"Couldn't sleep," she said, opening Lane's laptop, typing in her name as a password. The screen opened to a picture of their family at Matt and Alexandra's wedding.

She smiled as she checked search history, finding Todos Santos near the top of the screen. She leaned left, smiling at Eric looking out the front window. Christine searched 'Todos Santos,' then checked it out on the map before getting out a credit card.

Eric turned to her smiling. "Late night shopping?"

Christine nodded, beginning a WestJet search of available seats to San Jose, Cabos.

Alejandro cursed under his breath as he worked the hoe

between rows of bougainvillea and birds of paradise. His grey clothing and the brim of his ball cap were sticky with sweat.

The second advantage to his job was it allowed him to lose the weight he'd put on sitting in front of a computer through much of his teenage years. The first was hope.

Tio Victor, this had better work out as planned, he thought, standing, arching his back, thinking about how Tio Victor and General Rodriguez had worked out a plan to get the money back from all the wealthy fresas with their tax haven fortunes, putting the money back into communities.

Victor kept saying, "The more people sharing in the wealth, the better it will be for everyone."

"All I know is that I'm sick and tired of working as Senor Thomaso's gardener, handyman and property manager for $20 U.S. a day." This and three other properties kept he and his wife going, just. She worked at one of the resorts in members' services making less than he did, even during a good month when a commissions cheque arrived.

He leaned the hoe against a pillar, sitting on the front step of the 11,000 square foot mansion east of Cabo San Lucas. The white adobe style hacienda overlooked the Pacific.

Alejandro sipped a mixture of fresh lemon and water from his thermos, gazing over Thomaso's pool and past its palapa to the ocean where a cruise ship sailed south from the Cabo harbour.

It's time the pinche fresas paid their share, he thought as he had every day for five years. If all went as planned, he and Veronica would be moving within a month.

He turned around, looking through the glass into the sitting room and its custom-made furniture. He remembered Sra. Thomaso telling him how much they paid for the white leather couch and chair. It was more than they paid him in one year. It had taken a tsunami of self-control for him to smile and nod in admiration.

His phone rang, he pulled it from his pants pocket, peering through a cracked screen, seeing Veronica's number, pressing answer. "Hola."

"Te necesito." She choked out the words.

"Que pasó?"

"Ven aca." She hung up.

"I'm not going into Mexico without seeing you and your evidence. You are a ghost. I don't like ghosts." KG sat on the second floor of his log home in an easy chair with a view of Mt. Lemmon. "You want us to do this job? Then you need to show up."

Brenda sat with her blue bunny slippers, toes kissing each other on the coffee table. "What do you need exactly?" *Don't back off with this guy but do get some specifics.*

"I want to see the paper and your face so I know what you're telling me is the truth."

"I have copies of boarding passes and an email from Mexico City. Will that do?"

"Yes, bring them along."

"Where are you?" Brenda tucked the burner between her shoulder and ear while reaching for her regular phone.

"Tuscon. You know where that is?"

"Yep. Then I call you at this number?"

"Let me know when you're comin' and we'll work from there." KG hung up.

Brenda typed Tuscon into her phone, then used her burner to call Colin Wright.

He answered after the third ring. "What's up Brenda?"

"I need the company jet. They want me in Tucson."

"Hold on a minute." Colin covered the phone's speaker.

She waited, tapping the toes of her slippers together, doing a mental inventory of what she would need to pack.

Colin came back a minute later. "The jet's available at three this afternoon. You've been to the Executive Flight Centre before?"

"I know where it is. Who do I talk to?"

Rhonda tapped on Nigel's office door before opening it. "Colin Wright just got a call from a number on our list. It's a burner and it matches a number from his father's phone. We have a name."

Nigel looked over the monitor on his desk. The half-moons under his eyes were purple. "Okay?"

"Brenda B."

"On the Board of WTF?'"

Rhonda nodded, "Brenda Bruciarsi."

He turned his head sideways, watching her with one eye. "You've got to be fuckin' kidding me."

She shook her head. "Nope. One and the same."

He looked at the ceiling. "Now we know for sure she's tangled up in this."

"Hashir is getting a location on her as we speak. He asked me to ask you what you want done when he locates her?"

Nigel scratched the top of his head. "She's gonna need the full meal deal, which means I've got some paperwork and phone calls to take care of. Can you get Lori on the phone? The Chief's out of town, right?"

"Some conference in San Diego." She turned to walk out the door.

Nigel nodded, reaching for the phone. "We need to move fast. Bruciarsi has a knack for knowing when to leave just before 'shitaster' strikes."

She smiled, familiar with Nigel's obscene, often obscure adaptations of English. "That last one was a mouthful."

He dialed. "It sounded better in my head. I need to talk with Lane."

Her phone chirped. She stopped, reading a text, turning,

walking back into Nigel's office. "First, you're gonna want to know what Hashir just found."

The drive to San Jose took twenty minutes of passing tour buses and taxis along the winding four lane coast highway. Alejandro's red Ford Ranger was a decade old and on its second engine but he worried most about the fresa takeoff tires.

When he rounded the traffic circle to join Boulevard San Jose – four lanes paralleling the beach – he knew something major was happening. The eastbound lanes were a parking lot of buses, taxis and police.

He pulled over to the curb, parking, running along the sidewalk toward the Royal Luna where Veronica worked. He passed six resorts in five minutes before reaching the edge of a crowd blocking the boulevard.

Most of the people were women wearing the uniforms from various shops and all-inclusive resorts. They formed a wall of anger out front of the Royal Luna.

He climbed Luna's pink adobe wall, standing next to a palm tree, looking over a sea of black hair. The crowd blocked the front entrance of the resort. He spotted Veronica with her arms crossed, her friend Monica alongside.

"Grab him by the balls!" one woman shouted as a bearded man in a blue and orange tropical shirt and shorts stepped through the glass doors. He was towing his wheeled luggage. Alejandro estimated the man was between six and seven feet tall and over 300 pounds, his face a mask of arrogant defiance.

"Romper los huevos!" Two women chanted in stereo.

Others picked up the chant.

"ROMPER LOS HUEVOS!"

Alejandro realized he was witnessing a phenomenon he'd only seen on YouTube. It was called a 'Fiesta de Trumpos.'

The first spontaneous events like this had occurred in Playa del Carmen and then Cancun. Males accused of sexually assaulting resort employees were being shamed at an unprecedented rate.

At first, all-inclusive management defended offenders. Employees and guests soon convinced bosses to side with the women. The wealthy offenders (almost universally heavy drinkers of all-inclusive booze) who got handsy with female employees caused what could only be described as revolts.

Female employees and their male supporters, alerted by texts and social media, gathered around resorts until offenders were bounced from the hotels. The offenders were filmed and the events posted on social media.

"ROMPER LOS HUEVOS!" The chant was reaching a crescendo.

The fresa in the blue and orange shirt pushed his way through the crowd. He looked over his shoulder, spotting Luna's security blocking retreat through the glass doors.

The chant became a roar.

Women raised their fists.

The offender bent at the knees, forearm out front, forcing women out of his way.

A woman fell. Waiting police surrounded the man, escorting him through the crowd to a black and white pickup where he was handcuffed. They backed him up to sit on the tailgate.

The red and blue lights flashed as the police vehicle inched forward, its siren just audible over the women chanting, "ROMPER LOS HUEVOS!"

Minutes later, the crowd was dispersing as people returned to work. Alejandro was able to swim against the tide of bodies, finding his way to Veronica sitting in a wicker chair, drinking from a bottle of water.

She lifted her chin, a weary light in her green eyes as she recognized him, smiling through tears.

The first inkling about the problem in San Jose came from a video on social media.

Maria was wearing her immaculate camouflage pants, tan combat boots, black t-shirt, hair tied back with elastic. She sat outside under the awning, working on her laptop, looking up, waving Andreas over. As always, he was clean shaven and dressed in fatigues.

He stood behind her, putting a hand on her shoulder, leaned in close to the screen, pointing.

"Veronica." He waved Rodriguez and Lane over. "Ven aca. There was a 'Fiesta de Trumpos' at Luna in San Jose."

Lane brought his cup of coffee along as he looked over Maria's shoulder. "What's happening?"

Andreas said, "It appears a fresa sexually assaulted one of the women at Royal Luna and there was a demonstration. They have become quite common in Mexico. If a guest makes improper advances, there is a demonstration. He is kicked out of the resort and arrested."

Rodriguez said, "Si. I think you are correct. It looks like Veronica was assaulted. You must contact Alejandro now! He will want to go after the pendejo. Give him other options."

Andreas pulled his phone from his pocket, dialing, waiting as he held his index finger up. "Alejandro? Can you hear me?" Andreas waited, nodding at his grandfather. "Is Veronica safe?" He nodded at Rodriguez, smiling. "Good. We need her here. Can you bring her?" He listened. "Now. Today. We will have dinner for both of you." He waited, nodding. "Eso es bueno."

Andreas set the phone on the table, pressing 'end.' "They should be here in two or three hours." He looked at his watch. "As long as his truck does not break down."

Rodriguez nodded. "Then he needs a new truck."

Lane's phone rang. He picked it up off the table, pressing 'answer.' "Hey Nigel." He set it back on the table, putting it on speaker.

Nigel asked, "How are you doing?"

"It's beautiful, sunny, great food, better company. You?"

"Look. We've got a line on a connection to the Wright killing and the death of the contract killer. A phone number was found on both Wright's and Wilson's phones. It belongs to Brenda Bruciarsi. We are in the process of initiating surveillance."

Lane looked at Rodriguez who was frowning.

Lane said, "That is interesting. We are talking the Brenda Bruciarsi from the PMO?"

"That's her. Let Lauren know. Anything new at your end?"

"Something called a 'Fiesta de Trumpos' happened in San Jose today. It's created some tension here. I'm not exactly sure what the fallout will be."

"What kind of fiesta?"

"I just saw a YouTube video. It's a public shaming of a tourist accused of sexual assault."

"I'll take a look."

Lane spoke quickly. "How are Christine, Matt and the gang doing?"

"Well, as far as I know. Lori's got her people taking care of them. You know, no news is good news."

He nodded. "You have any information on the 45s?"

"The right wing white supremacist group in the States?"

Lane said, "Yes that's the one. We're getting signs they are getting ready to make a move. As of yet there are no indications about where, but it appears it will be soon."

Nigel said, "Good to know. I'll make our people aware here. Then I'll contact Keely. Can I get back to you?"

"Yes, please do."

Nigel hung up.

Lane looked at Rodriguez who sat across from him at the table under the awning. Andreas stood behind him. Lauren sat at the head of the table next to Maria.

Lane said, "It appears we may have another complication."

Maria asked, "Who is this Bruciarsi?"

Lauren said, "She's a Canadian; a woman who works in the shadows. She operated from Canada's Prime Minister's Office – we call it the PMO – and it was never made clear what her role was. Some called her a fixer."

Andreas asked, "What is this fixer?"

Lauren lifted her eyebrows. "She would handle problems, keep the Prime Minister away from scandals, get rid of people who could cause problems for the PMO, smooth talk the heavy weights from banks and corporations. It was all very vague and behind the scenes. There are two known photographs of her. Some called her the most powerful and most camera-shy woman in Ottawa."

Rodriguez nodded. "We have people like her in Mexico as well. Often they have connections to organized crime." He pointed at Lane. "And, we have had experience with another group like the 45s. Was it eight years ago?"

Maria pulled at her right earlobe. "You were the one who helped take down Los Macuahuitls?"

Andreas pointed at Lane and his grandfather. "We worked together with Nigel, Anna, and Arthur. It was very successful."

Rodriguez said, "Now we have this new problem with the 45s and their wealthy bosses."

Hashir watched Brenda Bruciarsi through a long Nikon lens. The flight attendant walked behind Brenda, pulling a white, black and yellow striped rolling trunk.

I'm sure her luggage costs more than a month's salary, he thought while pressing the shutter release.

Brenda strolled across the tarmac, wind blowing her hair sideways as she climbed the steps to board the white gold twin engine Bombardier Challenger executive jet.

He snapped several shots of the plane's C-WTFW

identification before reaching for his phone.

Lane noted the arrival of the red Ford pickup with peeling paint on a sun-scalded hood. He studied the driver's face, recognizing Alejandro, turning to study the slender woman sitting next to him. She wore a white blouse, had shoulder length black hair, Groucho Marx eyebrows and a smile.

Rodriguez stood on the patio outside the sliding glass door, his arms crossed, eyes on Alejandro as he climbed out.

Andreas leaned close to Lane. "My grandfather is worried Alejandro went after the pendejo fresa and that is why they are late. His wife's name is Veronica."

Veronica's door complained as she opened then slammed it. It popped back open. She leaned against it, holding the handle up, releasing it, ensuring it would stay closed this time. She looked at Lane and Lauren, before walking to Rodriguez. "We are late because I went to the police to file a complaint."

Rodriguez lifted his chin at Alejandro wearing grey coveralls who said, "There were four witnesses who had to write their statements."

Angela said, "You're just in time for paella. Wash up. Sit down. Talk as we eat."

Five minutes later Angela set a cast iron pan in the centre of the table atop a block of wood. "Probecho."

Lane looked at the yellow rice dotted with shrimp, clams, chorizo sausage and chicken. He closed his eyes, inhaling the blend of aromas, opening his eyes, realizing his appetite had returned. He looked across at Alejandro who was looking at the courtyard wall without seeing it.

Rodriguez lifted his chin at Veronica sitting alongside Alejandro who passed her husband's plate for Angela to scoop him a generous spoonful. Alejandro's focus followed the aroma as the plate was set before him. He picked up a fork, nodding at

Angela.

After each plate was filled and after Lane took the first bite of saffron spiced rice, he focused on Angela. She chewed slowly, studying the expressions of the people at the table. Conversation had died. Angela smiled.

Lane picked up a shrimp, tearing off its legs, then its exoskeleton, all the time watching Angela appreciating them appreciate the food.

Conversation began with second helpings and the deeper shades of colour from the evening sun.

Petra wiped her fingers with a paper napkin, turning to Veronica. "We saw the video from 'Solaris.' What happened?"

Veronica held a chicken leg between thumbs and forefingers. "One of the members was drunk. He came over, put his arm around my shoulder, then he grabbed my breast and tried to kiss me. I pushed him away, he came back, I slapped his face, he tore my blouse. Carlos and Mario pulled him away. He tried to fight them. Security was called. Then some people began to record him with their phones. He stopped. He pretended to be the victim. By then security and the manager arrived. After that I didn't see him until he was leaving. Now he's in a cell at the police station, complaining he's innocent and asking for help from the embassy."

Lane set his water glass down. "Where's he from?"

Alejandro glared. "Fucking Canadian."

Veronica tapped the table. "Toronto."

Lane looked at Lauren, she raised her eyebrows. "I'll ask Nigel to check on the suspect's background."

Veronica said, "I still feel kind of ashamed."

Petra pointed a fork at her. "What for?"

Veronica shrugged, blushing.

Lauren leaned back in her chair. "I felt the same way when it happened to me. That I had somehow given off the wrong signals."

"That is how it feels."

Lauren put her elbows on the table. "It was my graduation.

Things in the town had kind of gotten back to normal after my brother attempted suicide. I was asked to grad and went with one of the guys who was playing hockey for the Wolves. On the way home from an after-grad party, he offered a ride to one of the guys on the team. In the parking lot, they asked if I wanted a threesome. I told them no thanks, it was the wrong time of the month. They took me by the elbows and turned me upside down."

"Then?" Petra asked.

"I broke one guy's nose and the other's arm."

Rodriguez slapped the table with an open palm, smiling. "Perfecto!"

"Then?" Lane asked.

Lauren shrugged. "The boys went to the police. I spent the night in jail. My mom raised hell. I was released but the boys denied what they'd done and no charges were ever laid. I left town with my brother a month later to go to school in Calgary. Haven't been back since."

Alejandro put his cervesa down. "Did it feel good to beat those boys?"

Lauren shook her head. "Not really. I did it without thinking. I'd taken karate lessons. The training just kind of took over. Afterwards, I kept thinking I should have found a better way."

Lane wiped his fingers with a napkin. "Like what?"

She turned to him. "I don't know. Something that didn't involve violence I guess."

"I spent years wondering what I could have done so I wouldn't have to shoot a killer. I finally realized I did what needed to be done." He pointed at Lauren. "Just like you did what needed to be done." He pointed at Veronica. "Like the way the hotel kicked the pendejo out and arrested him. That is what needed to be done."

Rodriguez lifted his hands, palms facing the rest of the table. "And now, after years of planning, we are going to do what needs to be done." He turned to Alejandro. "I need you to check out some drones for me, por favour."

Rhonda walked across the office, leaning on the half wall of Hashir's cubicle, noting his closed eyes. She touched his shoulder. His eyes opened then he smiled.

She said, "Bruciarsi's plane is headed for Tuscon. Nigel says you have a few hours and he wants you to go home, see the family, get some rest."

Hashir nodded, looking at the time. "I can see the kids before they go to bed if I hurry. Is Nigel letting everyone know about Bruciarsi?"

"I will. Go home."

Lane's phone vibrated in his shirt pocket. The text read:
Bruciarsi headed for Tuscon. Suspect a meeting with 45s.
He stood up, going inside to find the Rodriguez.

Dan bent over, pulling back the covers on his side of the bed, groaning when his lower back gave him a painful reminder. As usual, the fourteen-hour film industry days of moving equipment, setting up a shot, focusing, doing it all over again had taken its toll. "Let me get this straight. Matt is taking time off. Alexandra is going to try and talk them into giving you more time off. I'm driving you to the airport in the morning. Your uncle has no idea you're on the way and you're not 100% sure you know where he is."

Christine pulled the zipper on Dan's black carry-on bag, setting it onto the floor next to the bed, climbing in on her side.

"Pretty much."

"And, one more time, please explain why you are going?" He walked over to the door, shutting off the light, returning to bed.

"It needs doing."

CHAPTER 9

Christine hefted her purse and school bag, leading the way out the back door followed by Dan carrying two black equipment bags. Rory watched out the kitchen window as they crossed the backyard and opened the garage door. Two minutes before, Rory had checked the garage, ensuring their safety. The kids were asleep upstairs, Alexandra had arrived earlier with Matt. Karen slept tucked in her portable car seat.

When Christine and Dan were buckled up inside their SUV, he opened the garage door, started the engine and backed into the alley.

"Say it."

He shook his head. "Say what?"

"That you think I'm crazy for going to bring him home."

"You're not crazy, you're just... "

"Go on." She looked left as he turned right, heading for 16th Avenue. Early morning traffic was light.

"Impulsive. You make impulsive choices. And once you make up your mind to do something impulsive, nothing can change your mind."

She looked right as they turned east onto 16th Avenue. "I left Paradise on an impulse. I found you on an impulse. I feel certain this needs to be done."

"Just make sure you both get home safe. Your uncle has a knack for getting himself into some dangerous fucking situations."

Alejandro and Veronica drove Rodriguez's air-conditioned pickup along the coast highway. She tapped the passenger glass window with her forefinger. "Ver las ballenas."

He leaned forward, looking at the Pacific where a pod of whales spouted. One came up out of the water. With three-quarters of its body was above the surface, it fell sideways into the ocean.

Louise rode a red fairway mower. She wore a yellow hard hat, jeans and work boots. The smell of fresh mowed grass filled her senses as she maneuvered along the edge of the rough at Calgary's Hawk's Nest Golf and Country Club. Estate homes dotted the perimeter of the eighteen-hole course touted as one of the world's premier destinations. Every August it hosted a PGA tournament to polish its profile.

The sun was up half an hour ago. Her kids were still a sleep at home with Louise's father Mark watching over them. They looked forward to Monday, Louise's day off, where they could have a barbecue on the two metre by two metre patio at the back of Mark's bungalow. They'd moved in two years ago after Louise's husband left for an acreage west of the city with his twenty-year-old girlfriend.

Louise topped a gentle rise in the fairway, spotting a blue four seat Gaia golf cart parked next to the green on the fifth hole.

She recognized Bill Shyne and his caddy. Louise eased off the accelerator, stopped, ducking down, shutting off the engine.

All maintenance employees had been warned Mr. Shyne would complain to management if he spotted any of the greens crew while he was golfing.

She looked west at the Rockies, glancing back every so often as Shyne putted, going back to his cart. He lifted his red cap. There was a gust of wind from the south. His strawberry blond comb over went north. Shyne swiped it south before slapping his cap back on.

Brian – Shyne's caddy and the club's pro – hefted the golf bag onto the cart. Every member of the maintenance crew knew to avoid Brian who bullied them all with impunity due to his exclusive relationship with Shyne.

Louise smiled. The six-day work weeks with mornings at the golf course and afternoons at the café might soon be coming to an end. There was a possibility of going back to school. A chance meeting with a woman named Anna could open a door for her and her kids.

She looked up as Mr. Shyne drove out of sight in a golf cart worth more than her car and tried unsuccessfully not to hate the arrogant son of a bitch.

Brenda Bruciarsi sat under the shade of an umbrella next to the hotel's pool. She wore white, sipping a mojito, eating huevos rancheros, waiting for KG to show.

He appeared, wearing a brown Tucson cowboy hat by Stetson. It was complemented by handmade gator cowboy boots, blue jeans and a red double-breasted canvas shirt.

If no one happened to notice his arrival, the spurs ensured a ringing proclamation.

He took off his hat, dropping it on the table across from her. The chair screeched on cement as he pulled it out, sitting, leaning back. "Welcome to Tucson, Miss B."

She sipped her mojito, licking her lips, extending the silence between them.

He lifted his arms to put his hands behind his head, losing balance, arms windmilling.

Brenda slammed her palms on the table. The toes of his boots caught the underside of the glass and she held it there until he regained his balance. Before he had time to establish composure she said, "You called this meeting." She reached into her purse, pulling out a manila envelope, tucking it under his hat. "The documents requested."

He took the envelope, lifting the flap, pulling out copies of emails and a photocopy from the Registro Catastral for a property in Todos Santos, Baja California Sur.

She said, "It's likely you'll find them there. It's an hour out of La Paz. If you go through Mexicali it's about 1,200 miles. The GPS coordinates are on the back of the document."

He flipped the paper over, checking, looking around. A family of four sat three tables over. Mother and father tried to eat while feeding twin two-year-olds. "Who are we after?"

Neither of them paid any attention to the Latina waitress surreptitiously photographing them with a phone camouflaged by a tray of empty glasses.

Brenda reached down and into her purse. "Photographs of the principals. Lauren Jackson is a Calgary detective and her accomplice, Paul Lane. Rodriguez, Mexico's Minister of Justice and his grandson Andreas, along with any and all other occupants."

She pointed her mojito at KG. "Your employers and mine are concerned the occupants are about to make another Panama Papers-style revelation. If that happens, a public outcry could force governments to demand lost tax revenues. This would conceivably cost your employers and mine $15 trillion or more. They want us to prevent such an outcome. You and your crew are tasked with the job. A one half of one percent commission on the $15 trillion will be your share." She waited for him to do the math.

He pulled a phone from his shirt pocket, punching numbers into the calculator, eyebrows rising at the answer.

"Anything else I need to know?"

"Our employers require photographs as proof. You can use your cellphone and forward them to this number." She held out her hand, taking his phone, entering the number under Miss B.

He took the phone back. "What is your cut?"

"Not your concern. Do you have a problem with your remuneration?"

He shook his head, standing, picking up his hat.

"Expect confirmation in two to three days."

Sitting next to the aisle near the rear of the plane, Christine closed her eyes. She listened to music from her phone, filtering out the snoring of the guy in the middle seat who sat knees wide apart, making her minimal space minuscule.

It was here at over 30,000 feet where the doubts began to tug at her confidence. Would she find the right bus to Todos Santos? How would she find her uncle once she got there? Would he even be there? Where would she stay tonight?

The uncertainty took her back to the predawn fears when she left Paradise with her belongings in a garbage bag, catching a ride to Calgary, being turned away by her Uncle Joseph. The panic of not knowing where her next meal would come from. Being taken in by Uncles Lane and Arthur. No questions, only hugs, good food, a warm bed.

It'll all work out. You'll find him. You know where to look. Just handle the problems one at a time. Just like Uncle Lane taught you.

She felt the engines throttle back. A moment later there was pressure on her eardrums.

The pilot announced, "We've begun our descent to San

Jose. It's currently 32 degrees and sunny. Thank you for flying WestJet."

Andreas saw his vibrating phone dancing on the table. He picked it up, reading a text from Enrique in Tucson. He tapped an image, enlarging it, walking outside to his abuelo. "We have a message and a photograph from Enrique."

Rodriguez looked up from his laptop. He was sitting under the awning, enjoying a coffee with Lane. "What is it?"

Lane set his coffee down on the table, brushing the crumbs from his shorts, listening.

Rodriguez took the phone. "This is Gumbay-Yaw, the leader of the 45s." He pointed an index finger at the image. "Who is the woman?"

Andreas shrugged. Rodriguez handed the phone to Lane.

"She does look familiar. Okay if I ask Lauren?"

Rodriguez said, "Of course."

Lane stood, taking the phone across to the gate where Lauren and Angela stood guard.

"Know who this is?" He handed the phone to Lauren. Angela leaned in to get a look.

Lauren said, "I think it's Brenda Bruciarsi." She pulled her phone out of the back pocket of her shorts, tapping the screen, swiping, holding the phones side by side. "Nigel sent this to me."

Angela said, "It is the same person."

Lane nodded. "What is she doing in Tucson meeting with the 45s?"

KG climbed down from his pickup. Chris Spicer waited nearby

under the shade of the Expedition's open rear hatch.

KG walked over, his spurs singing, kicking up dust. "I've called Joe and Rube. They're on their way." He looked at his watch. "We leave in an hour."

Chris said, "We're packed and ready. Your gear is here." He leaned inside, picking up a black backpack, handing it to KG. "Everything on your list."

He took the pack, hefting its weight, nodding "This job'll take a week or less."

Louise kicked off her boots. The toes were stained green. She unlocked the back door of her father's bungalow, heading downstairs to her bedroom. It was in between her children's rooms and across from the bathroom.

She stopped in front of the laundry room door, opening it, stripping off her clothes, stuffing them in the washer. Fifteen minutes later, she put on her white blouse and black slacks, combed out her hair, sneaked a peek at her sleeping kids then headed upstairs.

The coffee was on. She smiled while pouring it in her stainless-steel travel mug. She went into the front room where her father snored on the couch. She covered him with a quilt before going out the back door, heading to her second job.

Christine sat on the concrete bench out front of the blue and white bus terminal in San Jose. Her bags sat on either side as she sipped water, watching the traffic, looking up the hill to the white walls of the Walmart. She closed her eyes, savouring the Mexican sun.

She inhaled a combination of desert air, spent diesel fuel

and raw sewage wafting from the manhole five metres away. Her eyes opened, she checked her watch, wondering if the bus would be on time. Then she took the map from the side pocket of her purse to make sure she had some idea of where she would go when the bus arrived in Todos Santos.

Rube was about thirty-five, wore a MAGA ball cap, a black T-shirt, jeans and black S.W.A.T. tactical boots. His head and face were shaved, his cheeks sunken and top two front teeth missing. He had a prosthetic device he kept popping in and out of place as he tapped the screen of his iPad.

Chris had been driving for more than two hours on Interstate 8 bound for Yuma. KG was 200 yards ahead in his pickup. The beige of the desert was dotted with the intense green of irrigated farmland as they neared the Colorado River. He checked the outside temperature on the Expedition's dash. It was just over 100 degrees Fahrenheit.

Rube's bird voice was a magpie squawk. "What is KG up to?"

Chris shook his head, then opened his mouth to answer.

Rube said, "I know KG's story about us taking out kidnappers who snatch American kids is bullshit. What's the real story?"

Chris felt sweat trickling down his ribs.

Rube shook his forefinger. "Don't bullshit me. I've been checking up on your SEAL credentials while we've been driving. Did you know guys like me can check the SEAL database?"

The trickle of sweat rolling from Chris' armpits along his ribs was becoming a river. "Really?"

Rube lifted his cap, scratching his scalp. "There's no Chris Spicer in the database."

Chris nodded; eyes locked on the road ahead.

"Do you know how to shoot?"

"Of course!" Chris choked out the words.

"Here's the thing." He tapped the iPad. "If we're up against some vatos with AKs they're usually pretty disorganized. If we're up against something else, their special forces for example, I wanna know."

"If you don't trust KG, why are you here?"

Rube tapped the side of his head with his forefinger. "Trips like this one paid for my house." He tapped his front teeth. "And the dentist." He turned to face Chris. "KG, Joe and me been buddies since high school. Played football together. We know each other pretty well. I also know KG always looks out for himself first. Always has. Always will. Me..." He pointed at his chest. "I like to know what I'm getting into. So, here's the deal. I'll keep your little secret if you tell me what you know."

He waited, noting the growing patch of sweat under Chris's right arm.

"Yesterday he went to see this woman who came down from Canada. He called her Brenda something. Said she flew down the night before in a private jet owned by a company he called WTF. Right after meeting her, he called you and Joe. A day or two before that, he told me to get the equipment ready and the vehicles loaded up."

He looked right, saw Rube tapping in the letters WTF. "One other thing." Rube tapped 'enter.'

"What's that?"

"When we get there and go in after these vatos, you're gonna be out front of me, never behind." He looked at Chris, waiting for eye contact. "Got it?"

Chris nodded. "Yep."

Nigel and Anna's daughter Natalie knelt in a chair. Louise set Anna's pancakes on the table under the shade of a white umbrella. Anna had her blonde hair tied back in a ponytail. They were on the patio outside of 'The Café' where Louise worked the lunch crowd.

Anna said, "Thanks. How are you?"

Louise smiled. "Looking forward to Monday and some down time. How about you?"

Anna glanced at the pancakes. "Hungry. I love the pancakes." She began to cut them up, pushing the plate closer to Natalie.

"One of our best sellers."

Anna reached under the stroller, pulling out a manila envelope. "This is for you." She handed it to Louise. "S.A.I.T. runs a culinary arts program. You were talking about wanting to be a chef."

Louise smiled. "Very kind of you, but…"

Anna held up her hand. "I just thought you might want to look. There may be an opportunity for grants next week. It would cover tuition, books and living expenses for two years. It's a pretty generous plan actually. If you are a successful graduate, you are not required to pay it back. The only stipulation is that you help out by hiring another graduate within ten years of your completion of the program."

Louise looked toward 'The Café.' She used her free hand to wipe away tears. "Sorry."

Anna squeezed Louise's hand. "Take a look if you like. I'll be back next week. By then I should know if the grants are a go. Think about it."

Maria, Petra, Lauren, Veronica and Andreas gathered around Rodriguez. Lane came into the living area. Lauren waved him over. "You need to see this."

He walked out onto the patio. The midday sun beat the intensity out of the colours from the flowers in the garden. He put his sunglasses on.

Andreas moved to one side, allowing Lane a view of Maria's computer. There were pictures of a black Ram pickup and an Expedition.

Maria said, "Enrique sent us these pictures. KG and three men left Tucson, heading west. Two of the crew are familiar. They have travelled with KG before on missions into Mexico. Enrique managed to place a tracking device on the pickup." She tapped a key and a map of the southern Arizona appeared. She pointed at a green marker. "They are west of Yuma and approaching Mexicali. I will be watching their progress to see if they cross the border."

Rodriguez said, "We've anticipated this. Our main operation will continue as planned. If KG and his pendejos come for us, we will be ready." He tapped Maria on the shoulder. "Are we prepared for Sunday morning?"

She smiled. "Anna and I have everything nearly ready. There is one more back door to open. Anna has managed to find keys to all the others."

"Good. We need all of the doors open. Make that clear to her." Rodriguez turned to Lane and Lauren. "We should talk now."

Lauren asked, "Okay if I send the pictures of the 45s to my guys?"

Christine had one bag attached to the handle of her rolling luggage, pulling them up the hill past the playground and its palm trees. The wheels of her carry-on thumped over the cobbled street.

She stopped at the top of the hill, lifting hair from her shoulders, reaching into her pocket, pulling out an elastic, shaping her hair into a ponytail.

She looked left and right along Calle Benito Juarez. To her

right and across the street was a red adobe hotel. She waited for a couple of pickup trucks and a tour bus to pass before crossing the street and sitting on a bench out front of the hotel.

A man with a guitar stood under one of the hotel's arches singing, 'Welcome to the Hotel California.' His guitar case was open, anticipating tourist tips. He wore green shorts, a red T-shirt and dreads. She closed her eyes as he sang, hearing his American accent.

Christine opened her eyes, looking up the street at the 'Tequila's Sunrise Restaurant Bar' with its rusty red sign and patrons sitting out front on the broad sidewalk doubling as a patio. Her eyes tracked further up the street, spotting a round white sign with a coffee cup.

She stood, walking past the hotel's dusty parking lot, heading uphill until she stood in front of 'Cafelix Coffee'. She stepped down the ramp, spotted a table under a red umbrella and sat. To her left, a skeleton sat next to the entrance to the café and she smiled, certain her uncle would have visited this place.

For about five minutes, she watched the comings and goings of patrons who went inside before returning with drinks and/or food. She kept one eye on Calle Benito Juarez in case her uncle walked past. Then hunger made the decision for her.

Christine went inside, ordering three pescado empanadas and a latte. After paying, she went back outside to sit next to the skeleton, awaiting her order, planning her next move. She pulled out her cell phone, texting Dan and Alexandra.

Arrived Todos Santos. Found a coffee shop. Keeping an eye out for Uncle.

Joe drove the Ram pickup along Interstate 8. They were about 20 miles East of El Centro where irrigated fields turned the desert a lush green.

He turned his blue eyes right, seeing KG studying a map of Todos Santos. "So, what's the real story?"

KG folded the map, stuffing it in between the seat and the consul. He scratched his beard. "We never talked about your trip to Calgary."

Joe eased past a semi in the right lane, its eighteen wheels humming, making a response difficult. Once he was out front of the semi, he said, "Not much to tell. He didn't say much. Stuck a Beretta behind his ear, persuaded him to inject himself with insulin. It was all pretty standard." Paul felt no need to explain what he'd told Wright would happen to his grandchildren if he didn't comply.

KG nodded, looking out the window.

"Your turn. This job isn't about kidnappers is it?"

KG looked at Joe with that angelic face and blue eyes. KG stuck a thumb behind his belt buckle. "We're going to stop overnight in El Centro and get an early start tomorrow. Hungry?"

"I could eat."

Christine waited for the lady behind the counter to come out and take the dishes. The woman had short black hair and wore a white T-shirt, apron and jeans.

Christine lifted her chin. "That was very good. Gracias. Could I have another latte por favor?"

The woman smiled back. "Of course."

Christine took fifty pesos from her pocket. "I'm looking for my uncle. He's in his mid-fifties, has short grey hair and is missing part of his ear." She touched the gold stud on her earlobe. "Have you seen him?"

The woman smiled, shaking her head. "No." She took the dishes inside, leaving Christine to turn and watch the lazy procession of tourists, vehicles and a boy on horseback.

Hashir sat in front of his computer. He put two images side by side, manipulating them until they were the same size. Lauren had just sent the one on the right. It was the blonde member of the 45s. The image on the left was a passport photo of Donald Colton.

He looked back and forth between the images, checking eye colour, feeling the hairs on the back of his neck tingling. He stood up, turning toward Nigel's office, waving, getting Nigel's attention. "Boss! I've got an ID!"

Lauren's phone chirped. She sat outside at the table, enjoying the after-dinner glow of good food, sunset colours and a cold drink of water.

She read the message from Hashir, then stood up looking for Lane. He sat in the garden with Rodriguez who was talking on his phone, tapping Lane on the shoulder before waving Andreas over.

Lauren followed Andreas out and into the garden where Lane and Rodriguez were enjoying coffees. An emerald green hummingbird, not much bigger than a dragonfly, flew from one purple sage blossom to the next.

Rodriguez pressed end on the phone. "Gabriella says there is someone at Cafélix asking about Lane." He pointed at Paul sitting across the table, watching the hummingbird.

Lauren held her phone up. "I just got a message from Hashir in Calgary." She glanced at Andreas. "He is my partner investigating the death of Fred Wright. He has a passport photo of a person of interest in Wright's murder."

Lauren touched the face of the phone, bringing up Donald

Colton's passport photo. "This man was seen at Wright's building at the time of his death. He is also one of the men travelling with KG."

Rodriguez set his cup on the end table next to his chair before pushing himself to standing. "KG and his men are stopped in El Centro correct?"

Andreas nodded. "Yes."

"Then we deal with the immediate problem first." He put up his hand, waving Petra over. When she was within a couple of metres he said, "There is someone at Cafélix asking questions about us. I need you to go and have a coffee, then return with what you have learned. Bring back an image on your phone if possible."

Petra nodded. "I will change." She pointed at her military gear.

Christine looked down the street at the 'Hotel California'. *I wonder how much it costs for one night?*

A tall woman in a red dress walked through the patio gateway. Her long black hair rested on her shoulders. She walked past and inside.

Christine heard her say, "Dos cafés por favour."

Christine looked outside where the streetlights were beginning to come on. She looked at her bags, standing, hooking her purse over her shoulder.

The woman in the red dress said, "Espera un minuto." She set two coffees on Christine's table.

Christine looked at the latte, then looked inside the shop to see the woman behind the counter watching them. "Who are you?" Remembering a phrase Alexandra taught her she asked, "Quien eres tu?"

The woman tucked her dress under her bum, sitting, one leg crossed over the other, gesturing for Christine to sit. "We can use English if you like. My name is Petra."

Christine looked at the coffee, looked at Petra, then out onto the street. "The woman inside, she told you I was looking for my uncle."

"Her name is Gabriella and yes she phoned to tell us you were looking for the man with the missing..." She used a thumb and forefinger to wiggle her earlobe. "What is the word for this?"

"Earlobe."

Petra nodded, picking up her coffee, taking a sip.

Christine sat down, looking at her coffee, shrugging. "You are very direct."

Petra smiled. "Yes. You say this man is your uncle?"

"His name is Paul Lane. He is my uncle and he isn't expecting me." She took another sip of coffee before putting the cup down. "He looked after me when I needed help and now, I'm here to look after him."

"You say he is not expecting you?" Petra leaned back, flicking her hair off her shoulders.

"Yes. Can I be direct with you?"

Petra lifted her chin, smiling. "Please."

"I'm tired. I want to see my uncle. Obviously, you and Gabriella know where he is. I've never been good at playing games, so what is it you want from me?"

Petra set a small black bag on the table next to her coffee. She reached inside the bag, pulling out a phone, dialing. "Si. Yo hablar a Paul por favour?" She waited, watching Christine, lifting her eyebrows. "There is a woman here. She is about my height and her name is..." She waited.

"Christine." She held her hand out.

Petra said, "She wants to speak with you." She nodded, handing the phone across the table.

Lane asked, "Christine?"

"Hi uncle, how are you?"

"What the fuck are you doing here?"

Christine smiled. "It's good to hear your voice. We've been

worried about you."

Veronica lifted her eyebrows. She worked behind the counter in the members area of the Royal Luna. Two men and two women walked in. Both men wore shorts, wife beaters and sipped beer. The women wore battered cowboy hats, bikini tops and cut-off jean shorts. The guys leaned up against the desk.

The one with the red hair said, "We just need our room keys then direct us to the nearest bar."

Veronica smiled as his blond friend handed over their reservation. She entered the member number, glancing at the red head who sipped his beer and kept his eyes moving from her green eyes to her breasts and back. She asked, "You are?"

"Robbie." He lifted his beer, draining it.

She set up the door keys, sliding the cards into sleeves, writing the room numbers on them.

Robbie leaned closer.

She caught a whiff of secondhand alcohol and after-shave. Her eyes watered. She leaned away. "Your keys."

Robbie said, "You have amazing green eyes."

"Have a good visit." She smiled, letting her breath out slowly as the four took their keys, heading for the bar. She remembered what it had been like living in Sinaloa, her town infested with narcos. Some of the boys she went to school with joined the cartel because of family connections or because of the allure of money and machismo.

She looked right out the window, over the pool and to the ocean, reminding herself that life in San Jose was better than the life she left behind.

Her eyes returned to the swim up bar, halfway along the pool running down the middle of the resort. She saw the members who spent their days under the shade, drinking the hours away, wondering if Robbie and his group would do the same.

Veronica turned back to the computer, opening a private file, adding a paragraph.

The door next to the gate opened, revealing a bungalow and a lush garden of tropical colours. Christine stepped inside, inhaling the mixed floral perfume, closing her eyes. She felt herself wrapped in a hug, her uncle's familiar scent, his cheek against hers.

Lane asked, "How the hell did you find me? Why did you come here?"

Christine heard Petra's voice dance with laughter when she said, "A detective who misses the obvious. Christine loves you. She is worried about you. She is here."

Christine opened her eyes, adjusting to the faces nearby.

Lauren tapped Lane on the shoulder. "She must be tired and hungry."

A woman with black hair tied back in a bun wore camouflage pants and a grey T-shirt. She took Christine's bag. "My name is Angela. This way. We have plenty of food."

They met in KG's stainless steel, dark oak and granite appointed suite. They gathered around a table with two maps. One was a road map and the other a satellite photo. They each held a beer, Rube watching KG, Joe leaning back, Chris intent on the topography of the satellite map.

KG tapped the satellite map. "We come in from the North on Highway 19, turn left at the distillery here." He pointed at a dirt road winding through a stand of trees. "We take a right at the T intersection and stop right here."

He pointed at a bend in the road. "The trees will give us cover. The target is less than 100 yards through here." He put his finger on a bungalow at one end of a walled compound. "The walls are eight feet high." He pointed at Chris. "That's why we brought the collapsible ladders."

Rube set his beer atop the distillery on the satellite map. "What time do we hit them?"

Joe said, "Dawn is best. They'll just be waking up or still asleep. Good visibility is an asset when the terrain is unfamiliar."

KG nodded. "Rube and Chris will take this corner of the wall. Joe and I will go over the other. That way we can concentrate our firepower here." He pointed to the patio outside the kitchen.

Joe turned to KG. "Are we supposed to bring back any intel?"

KG shook his head. "We hit them hard, ensure all threats are eliminated then we withdraw." He moved Rube's bottle, setting the road map on top of the satellite. "We have two routes out. Back the way we came is primary. South to Cabo is secondary. I'm not expecting any complications, so we'll probably use the primary."

Joe asked, "How many targets do we have?"

KG sat back, resting his beer on his belt buckle. "Maximum of ten."

Rube rubbed his chin. "How many armed and how experienced?"

KG shrugged. "At least one of them is in his sixties. Expect some women as well."

Joe smiled. "Easy. In and out in five minutes." He held up an open hand for effect.

KG said, "After the threats are neutralized, I take a video with my cell phone for confirmation."

Joe slapped his thighs. "Looks good to me." He stood. "I'm gonna get some sleep."

CHAPTER 10

Christine asked, "Does she make these every morning?" devouring her second churro. "They are delicious." She pointed at her uncle and Rodriguez meeting in the garden. "Do they meet every morning?"

Lauren popped the last of a churro in her mouth, chasing it with a gulp of coffee, covering her mouth. "This is the first time for the churros and yes, they go out to sit in the garden every morning. I don't know what they talk about, but those two seem to enjoy each other's company."

Christine pulled another chair closer, resting her feet on it before cradling her coffee. "You know how those two met?"

"Not all the details."

"My uncles were in Cancun for Nigel and Anna's wedding. You ever heard of the Cipriani Scandal and a guy called Ben Poilievre?"

"Everybody in the CPS has heard about Poilievre."

Christine pointed her coffee mug in the general direction of her uncle. "Ben Poilievre was supposed to be dead, but he was living in Cancun and my uncle just happened to be nearby when Poilievre was murdered. It created a big mess. Rodriguez was sent to clean it up. He arrested my uncle and Nigel at his wedding as part of the investigation. Have you seen Nigel and

Anna's wedding pictures?"

Lauren shook her head. "No."

"There are shots of Rodriguez and his armed guards taking my uncle and Nigel away. Do you know that my uncle saved Rodriguez, Nigel and Andreas's lives by winging a guy who shot an RPG at the Hummer they were in?"

Lauren leaned closer, elbows on knees.

"After that, Rodriguez saw my uncle in a different light. At least that's what Nigel told me. A couple of years before that both my uncles helped set up some kind of trust for people in San Jose Cabo when they uncovered a fortune in drug profits. They worked with some of the locals to set aside money for schools and medical facilities. My Uncle Arthur told me about it. Uncle Lane made some very powerful enemies as a result."

Lauren pointed in the direction of Rodriguez. "And some powerful friends."

"Right now, it's the enemies I'm worried about."

"Actually, I'm glad you brought that up. It looks like there's trouble coming." She pointed in the direction of Lane and Rodriguez. "I'm pretty sure you are their topic of discussion and we're short of people."

Christine stood, looking down at Lauren. "I've learned if I'm the topic of conversation, it's time to join the discussion." She hefted her chair. "You comin'?"

Lane glared at his niece as she set her chair between he and Rodriguez. She sat down, waiting for Lauren to sit across from her.

Rodriguez interlocked his fingers under his chin. "Buenos dias."

Lane watched Christine as he sipped his coffee.

Christine turned to Rodriguez. "What do you need me to do? You might as well put me to work while I'm here." She looked over her shoulder at Maria who stood guard at the front gate. "You have four soldiers and two police officers. That means six people who can handle weapons." She turned back to Rodriguez. "And I bet you know how to handle a weapon. I heard someone talking about quatro gringros in Mexicali. I assume they are headed this way. That's what I've managed to pick up so far. What else are you willing to tell me?"

Rodriguez smiled at Lane. "You were right. Una mujer formidable." He turned to Christine. "You are a complication. I am trying to decide if that is a good thing or not."

Lane said, "The next 24 to 48 hours are going to be incredibly dangerous. I am still angry at you for showing up here."

Christine sat back in her chair, staring at her cup, then at her uncle. "You're just gonna have to get over it. I'm leaving when you leave." She turned to Rodriguez. "Put me to work. What do you know about these gringos? I have some experience with sociopaths. I may be of help there. And, I do know how to shoot. The gringos are coming from the States. It's an easy assumption they will be well armed."

Rodriguez asked, "Have you ever been shot at?"

Christine shook her head, attempting to hide her anxiety by taking a slow sip of coffee.

"It is very difficult to know how you will react in a situation if you have not experienced it before."

Lauren said, "I've been meaning to talk with you about that. I have studied the map of Todos Santos, our defences, the highway into town. I think it is possible to predict their approach and attack them first."

Lane leaned forward. "Okay?" He looked at Rodriguez.

The general stifled a smile. "What is your plan?"

Nigel sat at their kitchen table having breakfast with Natalie. The cabinets were white. He and Natalie sat at the island with its quartz countertop. Nigel had a tea towel tucked under his chin on the off chance Natalie decided to check out her arm by hurling a blueberry.

Anna came into the kitchen. "Good morning you two."

Nigel said, "I had an epiphany."

She opened the fridge, pulling out a jug of orange juice.

"We've been gathering evidence on a case, and this morning in the shower it all came together." He popped a strawberry in his mouth, chasing it with a sip of coffee. "Lane's been sending me texts. He knows most of what Rodriguez is up to, except he's been wondering about all the secrecy over the end game. It's very need to know. You know what I mean?"

Anna poured orange juice into a glass she'd bought on their last trip to Mexico. "And?"

"You've been very busy this last year – especially the last month or so – working on a project."

Anna watched him as she drank her juice.

"Maybe it's been longer than that. In fact, it goes back to 2016, November, I think. Then I remembered a certain 'Access Hollywood' tape and how you did so much thinking for about a week afterward."

Anna set her glass down. "Asshole got elected even after saying that about women. That's when I started thinking about doing something about it." She watched her daughter.

Nigel looked at Natalie, who popped a blueberry in her mouth. "How much can you tell me?"

"We have eyes on the guys going after Lane and Rodriguez. That information is continuously updated and passed on to Todos Santos."

"And?" He looked at Natalie who was trying to insert a blueberry into her ear. He reached out, pulling her hand away.

"If all goes well on Sunday, I can explain. Can you wait until then?"

The 45s stopped at the Pemex in San Felipe for fuel, then for some food just off the highway at a picnic table under the shade of interwoven palm leaves. The street vendor made burritos and tacos over a wood stove near the white sands of the Sea of Cortez.

KG stuffed the remainders of his first burrito into his mouth, moving the food into one cheek, swigging from his beer. "I can't wait to get back home and tie into a steak or burger."

Chris Spicer looked back at the SUV and the pickup. The heat rising from the hoods distorted the sunburnt hills on the inland side. He couldn't remember ever having a better taco.

Rube pointed at KG. "When we get back, you're buying the steak. Mine's gonna be rare."

Joe looked out over the water. "We stop in La Paz tonight. Maybe there will be a steak restaurant there. It's always easier doing a job after a good meal."

KG picked up another burrito. "After our targets are neutralized, you'll have your steak."

Joe pointed at Rube. "KG got word some of our targets could be female."

Rube lifted his chin. "White or dark meat?"

Joe smiled. "Maybe a bit of both."

Rube lifted his beer, waiting to touch glass with Joe. "We got us some fringe benefits."

Chris stared at his taco, realizing he wasn't hungry anymore.

Anna sat alongside her custom-built CPU. Her 34-inch curved monitor was cluttered with five separate websites.

The taped, sanded, unpainted basement drywall was wallpapered with pictures of Natalie and Nigel. Natalie slept behind her mother in a bed with a mobile of planets circling the sun. Anna's office was the coolest room in the house.

Anna had her hair tied back, keeping it safe from wiry tiny

fingers. She frowned, looking left on her desk where she kept red, white and green folders with the essential documents from federal, provincial and state governments necessary for the operation of IVB, their International Virtual Bank.

She turned back to her screen, bemused by the elusive back door solution to the final piece of the puzzle. One offshore banking system was becoming a disaster to master. It was a domino she would tip on Sunday, setting off a spiral chain reaction, opening the big money at the centre of each bank where the Untouchables hid their fortunes.

Natalie rolled over, sighing as Anna's mind nibbled around the edges of a solution to the final problem and the key domino.

Christine chopped carrots and celery for Angela who was in the process of disassembling and cleaning an assault rifle and a handgun. *What do I say to Dan? I promised to text him at least once a day. I'm helping prepare a meal while a woman cleans her weapons in anticipation of an attack?*

Christine focused on the knife while cutting two carrots into disks. She held the blade of her knife still, hearing the slick sound of machined metal as the components of the assault rifle clicked together in Andrea's practiced hands.

Brenda Bruciarsi drove the golf cart alongside the fifth hole of Hawk's Nest Golf and Country Club. She, Colin Wright and Bill Shyne existed in a weed free world of green.

Shyne wore a black golf shirt, red pants and red and white tailor-made golf shoes. His red ball cap appeared to be stapled to his strawberry blond comb over. "How come you wear this?"

He reached over, rubbing the white mesh of Brenda's head-to-toe mosquito netting covering blue pants and a violet long-sleeved blouse. He sniffed. "Isn't the mosquito repellent working?"

Brenda stopped the cart, lifting her hands from the wheel, counting off the fingers on her left. "Zika, dengue fever, malaria, West Nile, encephalitis. To name a few."

Colin Wright wore royal tartan pants and shoes. He looked around, ensuring no other golfers were within earshot. "Where are we with KG's team?"

Shyne stepped out of his side of the cart, leaning on the roof, waiting for Brenda to speak.

Brenda put her hands back on the wheel. "You don't want to know."

Shyne freed one hand to point at her. "It's our money," he pointed at Colin then at himself. "So we get to know. I have international partners who are asking. They require reassurance that the situation is in hand."

Brenda looked at them in turn, running her tongue over her front teeth. "KG and a team of three are headed for Todos Santos. They are tasked with eliminating the threat there."

Colin said, "This will repair the damage done by the Singer screw up?"

She nodded. "Absolutely."

Shyne rubbed his thumb and forefinger on the brim of his cap. "In specific detail, explain the threat in Todos Santos."

Brenda lifted her chin. "A Calgary detective and Mexico's Minster of Justice are involved in an investigation into the death of Mexican hacker Villanova and the attempt on Singer. Eliminating the Todos Santos threat and planting cocaine on the premises will muddy the waters and protect your assets."

Colin stepped out of the cart, moving around back, pulling the driver from his bag. "You trust this KG? His guy killed my old man."

Brenda turned to her right. "That's why I trust him. His guy got the job done without linking anyone to the job."

Shyne followed Colin to the back of the cart. "How much are we betting on this hole?"

Louise was on her way back to the maintenance shack when she spotted Bill Shyne's golf cart. She parked the mower behind a hedge, lifting her hard hat, wiping a sleeve across her forehead. Louise leaned forward, focusing on a man she didn't recognize. He wore loud pants. Then she spotted a figure wearing what might have been a beekeeper's outfit.

When Louise realized what she was seeing, she smiled. This course used a shitload of pesticides and herbicides. The chances of seeing a mosquito were about as good as winning a Lotto 6-49 jackpot. She glanced at her watch. She would have to hurry to get home, and then to work at the Cafe´.

Shyne and the guy in the loud pants got out of the cart, chatting before teeing off. She waited for them to move out of sight before turning the key, restarting her mower, leaning forward. Louise spotted two people wearing green and grey camouflage about 50 metres from Shyne. One held up a clear plastic parabolic listening device while the other watched the trio through a pair of binoculars.

Louise shook her head. *I hope they're getting something on Shyne to put him away.* She turned left, heading for the maintenance shed.

Anna shielded her eyes with her right hand as Natalie went the wrong way up the slide. They were in Bowness Park, where children played at the multi-coloured playground.

Natalie wore her polar fleece lion suit, tail wagging in the west breeze running down from the Rockies. She topped the slide, heading for the pole where she could slip to the ground and begin the process again.

Anna said, "Wrap your arms around the pole."

Natalie's eyes were focused on the task ahead of her, leaning forward, paws wrapping around metal, legs following, sliding to the ground.

Anna had her arms out in case of a mistake, but her daughter brushed protective arms away, heading for the slide.

The epiphany was very close to a smack at the back of the head. *I've been thinking horizontally instead of vertically. A backdoor isn't working, but a trap door or access though the attic should.* She stumbled back, closing her eyes. *It will work!*

"Natalie, it's time to go home."

The lion shook her mane. "No way!" She ran across the green bridge, heading for the cargo net.

Anna gave chase while the lion began laughing in a delicious game of catch-me-if-you-can.

The sun was high and the air still. Lauren Jackson's phone vibrated. She pulled it from her pocket as she stood outside the doorway to Rodriguez's compound.

It was her turn for guard duty. She'd borrowed a floppy, camouflaged cap from Andreas and wore the boots he had given her. The Mexican sun reminded her of the August Saskatchewan suns she'd known growing up.

Lauren stepped under the shade of a jacaranda tree so she could read a message from Rhonda.

RCMP confirms Todos Santos is target for 45s. Recording of conversation attached to email.

Lauren looked left and right. The street was virtually empty of traffic as people looked for a patch of shade or went to the beach to cool off. She walked over to the door, making a fist, pounding on the wood.

A minute later Andreas opened the door, handing her a bottle of water. "Agua?"

She took the bottle in her right hand while waving the phone with her left. "I need to see your abuelo."

He lifted his chin, plucking his hat from Lauren, taking her place outside.

Lauren looked around the gardens and the eight-foot cinder brick walls surrounding them, predicting the initial point of the attack.

She found Lane and Rodriguez in the garden being dive bombed by a hummingbird. They turned. Rodriguez wore a straw hat and Lane a grey Blue Jays ball cap. She held up her phone. "The attack is confirmed. There is a tape we need to listen to."

She turned, they followed her to the kitchen where she opened her laptop. Maria, Angela, Petra and Christine sensing urgency, gathering around. Lauren opened her laptop, maxing the volume so they could all hear the conversation between Bruciarsi, Wright and Shyne.

Lane pointed an index finger at the ceiling after the recording. "This Colin Wright is the son of Freddy Wright?"

Lauren nodded.

Angela asked, "So the son is working with the people who killed his father?"

Lauren nodded.

Rodriguez took his wide brim straw hat off before looking at Lauren. "We follow your plan." He looked at the people around the table. "Is everyone clear on their jobs?"

Christine raised her hand. "I'm not."

Rodriguez glanced at Lane before locking on Christine. "You will work with Maria. Is this agreeable?"

Christine stared back at him, waiting.

"His life,–" he pointed at Lane, then everyone at the table "–all our lives depend on each one of us knowing our jobs."

Christine nodded. "Okay."

Rodriguez looked at Maria.

"It is time to prepare the drones."

Maria nodded as she stood, heading for the storage shed.

Lauren looked at Christine who smiled, winking at her as the detective headed for the bathroom.

Lauren's phone chirped while she sat on the toilet admiring the multicoloured tiles on the walls and floor.

Lauren reached down, pulling the phone from her pocket, reading a text from Anna.

The attic hatch is open. We are a go for Sunday.

Lauren set the phone next to the sink, wondering what exactly Anna had managed to do. The years of planning and manoeuvering around roadblocks might actually amount to something tangible. She felt a thrill of anticipation, pushing it aside, focusing on the impending attack.

They sat at a red table in a room with a white, vaulted ceiling. According to KG, the restaurant was the best rib place south of the border. He'd ordered a full rack of pork ribs for each of them.

Joe insisted on two bottles of Casa Cortez. He rubbed his hands. "Best Mexican tequila."

Thirty minutes later, Chris looked at the clear liquid in the shot glass. He felt sweat gathering along his hairline and down his spine.

Rube put his hand on Chris' shoulder. "Bottoms up buddy. You'll sleep better and tomorrow morning you'll be in a mood."

Being in a mood – at least according to KG, Joe, and Rube – was required when they went into Todos Santos in the morning.

Joe leaned in close, wiping pork juice and barbecue sauce off his lips, whispering in Chris's ear. "For hundreds of years, warriors like us have been going into battle either drunk or hungover. It's a mean fuckin' way to fight. When the battle's over we go and tie another one on to celebrate."

Joe tapped Chris's temple with a forefinger. "My grandpa called himself a berserker. He fought in Italy during the war. Said they always got liquored up before a battle. It makes us part of a blood spilling tradition snowflakes can't even begin to understand. It's something a SEAL like you knows all about, I figure." He refilled his glass with more tequila.

Chris smiled, warm with liquid confidence, nodding, reaching for his glass, bringing the tequila to his lips, savouring its hot smooth passage down his throat.

Maria tapped the smartphone under the shade of the awning. The four propellers of the black drone became a bee swarm of sound. She took the drone for a quick flight around the gardens, checking its systems before bringing it back to land on the table. She shut off the motors, attaching its charger.

Maria turned her dark eyes on Christine, picking up a second controller. "I need you to operate this," she slid the tablet over, pointing at four split screens. "And learn to fly."

Christine leaned over the tablet. Her hair fell across her face. She reached into her shorts pocket, pulling out an elastic, tying hair back. "What do you need me to do?"

Maria leaned in close. "See this red arrow right here?"

Christine nodded. "Okay?"

"When I say now, you tap it, then get ready for the next move."

Christine looked around the table at the trio of black dragonfly drones and one smaller white drone. "You can fly all four at once?"

Maria shook her head. "No. That is why you need to learn how to fly."

Christine shook her head. "My son always beats me at video games. I'm hopeless."

Maria slid a smartphone next to the tablet. "You need to practice. Blanco, the white one, is easiest to fly. You just need to tell it where you want it to go." She tapped the image on the smartphone. The white drone powered up.

"You tap the screen and it goes to the spot you've chosen." Her finger hovered over the image of the property, tapping the image of a bougainvillea near the middle of the yard. The drone spun up, lifting off, flying to the centre of the property, hovering about two metres above the blossoms.

Christine thought, *I wish Indy or Ella were here. They would have no problem with this.*

She took the control in her hands, tapping the screen. The white drone dove into the bougainvillea.

Maria stood, indicating Christine should follow. "Every one of us is required to do a job when the 45s come. You will practice until you are proficient."

Christine inhaled, letting her breath out slowly. She'd noticed how direct, specific and insistent Maria's tone was and decided, *I can do this. I have to do this.*

An hour later, Maria said, "Okay, now you need to drop cans of beans on targets."

Christine frowned. "Did you say cans of beans?"

Maria nodded, holding up a can, attaching it to the cradle under the drone. It took another hour to become proficient at dropping the cans around the inside of the compound before stopping to recharge the drones.

Alejandro was finishing up for the day at the Thomaso estate. A pair of crystal white Cadillac Escalades arrived.

Gloria Thomaso stepped out of the first Escalade, followed by her personal trainer and dietitian. Gloria wore blue slacks and top, had her blonde hair tied back. She smiled at Alejandro. "We decided to fly down for the weekend." She turned as her children got out of the second Escalade with their twenty-something governess who wore pink yoga gear and a smile at least as bright as Gloria's.

Trina, her nine-year-old daughter, continued to play on her phone as she followed the governess through the front door. Dark haired, seven-year-old Mark ran over and hugged Alejandro around the waist.

Gloria said, "Mark was so excited to come and see his friend."

Mark asked, "You'll be around tomorrow?"

Alejandro said, "In the morning." He watched as the drivers unloaded the luggage. He looked at Gloria. "Everything is ready for you."

Mark said, "You got a new truck. I like it. What year is it?"

"It's from the '70s. Like new. Runs good."

"Can you take me for a ride?" Mark asked.

Gloria said, "Come on Mark, we have to get unpacked. We have dinner reservations in San Lucas."

Mark shrugged, following his mother inside.

Alejandro walked to his truck, feeling the weight of guilt like a bag of cement on his shoulders. By the end of the weekend, Alejandro knew Mark would be in for some difficult times.

Louise listened as the washing machine spun. She sat cuddling with her fifteen-year-old daughter Stephanie.

When Steph was a toddler, they would sit and watch TV together. Nowadays cuddling with Steph was a biannual occurrence. Louise was set on making this time last as long as possible.

Her knees were sore after a morning on the mowing machine and an afternoon on her feet, but she couldn't move for fear of disturbing Steph who'd broken up with her boyfriend last weekend and finally told her mother about it. Grandpa and Louise's twelve-year-old son Robert were watching the baseball game upstairs because mom and daughter required alone time.

Steph had tearfully confessed how Mark had told her he was going out with her former best friend Darlene. Stephanie's intense sense of betrayal and rejection was amplified by her age, the fact it was her first break up and being estranged from her father.

Louise looked at the walls. Baby and toddler pictures of her kids hung there. The TV rested atop a pair of red and blue plastic crates. Her feet rested on a plaid garage sale ottoman. They sat on the matching couch.

She shook her head at all that had happened to her life; the end of a marriage, moving in with her dad, working two jobs, trips to Value Village and trying to hold together what was left of her family. Watching it morphing into something different, hoping different would eventually prove to be better.

CHAPTER 11

Chris Spicer wore his combat gear. The acetaminophen had taken the edge of his headache and the bananas helped settle his stomach.

Still, he swallowed hard, leaning over, turning the Expedition's air conditioning to MAX. Rube sat in the passenger seat eating roadkill jerky. At least it smelled like roadkill. Chris was sure it had been immersed in a vat of garlic before being smoked with mesquite. The one blessing was the 50-mile drive from La Paz had been relatively free of traffic. They'd left just after five that morning.

An invisible toxic fecal cloud of sulphur filled cabin. Chris blinked, turning to a grinning Rube who said, "Wondered when you'd get a whiff. Like my brand?"

Chris dry heaved. "Open the fucking window next time you shit yourself!"

Rube pointed along the stretch of two-lane highway. "We're there. Watch for the distillery, take a hard right."

Chris looked down the road as the sunrise breathed colour into palm trees, hills and farms. On the right he spotted a white adobe building, partially covered with vines. He lifted his foot off the accelerator.

The screen on Maria's laptop captured the Ram pickup as it drove along the dirt road, kicking up dust. It was followed by an Expedition.

She waited five seconds before lifting the drone up off the top of the container, following the vehicles along the twin tracks in a dirt road flanked by palm trees. They turned right at a T-intersection.

She gained altitude, flying overtop the trees, seeing the walls of Rodriguez's compound through a gap in the green. Maria stayed 100 metres to the rear of the Expedition, setting the drone to hover. She spoke though her headset and microphone, remembering to use English in order to avoid confusion.

"Targets arrived. Stationary, 50 metres east of compound walls." She turned to Christine sitting across from her at the table under the awning. "Be ready. Things will happen very fast. Remember, we must hit them first."

Lauren wore camouflage gear, green paint on her face, tactical headset and a black cap. She shouldered the Xiuhcoatl assault rifle, nodding at Angela who stood across from her just visible behind the trunk of a palm tree. Angela lifted her chin, pointing her Xiuhcoatl in the direction the impending assault.

They knew Petra and Andreas would be ready about 60 metres south of them near the other corner of the compound wall.

Lauren flicked the safety off, aiming at the wall, waiting for targets to appear.

Chris opened the back hatch of the Expedition, sliding the SAW out, putting on his bulletproof ammo vest with four clips in the front pouches.

Rube took his Colt, putting on his vest, sliding a Glock in its holster. "Remember, you stay out front of me."

Chris nodded, stepping around the side of the Expedition. KG and Joe armed themselves with assault rifles and handguns. KG put on his vest.

Joe lifted his chin, moving to the back of the truck, pulling out an extendable ladder, waiting for Rube to do the same. Rube hefted the ladder in his free hand. Joe pointed to the right, indicating Chris and Rube take their prearranged position at the northeast corner. Then Joe pointed at himself and KG before heading to the southeast corner.

Both pairs moved toward their respective positions as they followed pathways in between palm trees.

Maria hovered 100 metres out, following their progress, using the zoom on the drone's camera. Christine followed Maria's progress on the laptop, monitoring the cameras, seeing the men separate into two groups.

Maria said, "Targets now two threats headed for the northeast and southeast corners of the wall." She lifted her eyes, looking at Christine. "Not yet."

Christine's fingers hovered over the face of the smartphone, preparing to send her drone into the air.

Lane and Rodriguez were inside the wall on either side of a bougainvillea at the centre of an X drawn from the four corners of the compound. Both had Xiuhcoatl assault rifles on their laps and extra clips tucked in their jacket pockets.

Rodriguez said, "I always instruct my soldiers to strike first. This is essential."

Lane nodded, watching the line of the east wall and its background of palm trees, anticipating the appearance of silhouettes. He moved forward off his chair, resting his elbow on one knee, steadying his aim.

Rodriguez remained seated, waiting, weapon pointing at the sky.

Rube and Chris reached the northeast corner of the eight-foot wall.

Rube began extending the ladder. "Watch our six."

Chris turned his back to the wall, pointing the SAW in the direction they had come, listening, hearing the sound of aluminum locks clicking into place.

Rube said, "Ready."

Chris turned, looping the SAW's strap around his right shoulder, climbing the ladder, reaching the top, hearing a buzz, dismissing it as insects.

Maria lifted her chin as she and Christine aimed their drones at separate corners of the compound.

Christine focused on the top rung of the ladder at the northeast corner. She saw the figure at the top, his black bullet proof vest, the weapon on his back. Her finger tapped between his shoulder blades. She watched the drone approaching the point, hovering about five metres above it.

Maria said, "Ahora!" Then, "Now!"

Christine turned from the phone to the tablet, watching the canister drop on the back of the man atop the ladder. The canister bounced off him, dropping to the foot of the ladder. The screen flashed white.

She heard the explosion, closely followed by a second. Christine looked to the far end of the compound.

Chris felt something hit his back, seeing the canister fall to the ground. The explosion at the foot of the ladder was a disorienting flash of white lightning and an immediate blast of sound. He tumbled forward, over the wall, headfirst onto a boulder.

Joe recognized the drone's buzz. He rolled face first on top the wall, right arm hanging down, left under his chin. Joe let his feet swing down the far side of the wall, extending his arms, dropping to the ground, sheltering from the blast on the other side.

Christine and Maria monitored the scene from about ten metres above ground.

Maria said, "Two down on your side. One down over the northeast corner."

Christine spotted movement. She set the drone to hover at the midpoint of the east wall. "One target moving along the south wall toward Lane and Rodriguez."

Maria looked at Christine. "Stay on him. I'll watch the east wall."

Lauren and Angela were separated by five metres, weapons trained on the man on the ground. He rolled over onto his belly, rising to hands and knees. Angela lifted her chin.

Lauren shouldered her rifle, drawing her Glock, putting her knee in the man's back, pistol at the base of his skull.

"Hands behind your back." She pulled a plastic double restraint from the clip at her waist, shoving her knee hard into the space between the man's shoulders, realizing he was deaf from the stun grenade.

She holstered her Glock, twisting one of his hands back, securing it in the restraint, grabbing the other wrist, zipping it tight. She stood up, leaning over the man, pulling the handgun from his leg holster, picking up his Colt assault rifle, nodding at Angela who lifted her chin at the ladder.

Lauren listened as Andreas said, "One secured. One over the wall." She handed the Colt to Angela then moved to the ladder, climbing, reaching the top. She peered over the edge, spotting the body at the bottom of the wall, its head at an impossible angle to the shoulders, eyes open, staring. She waited in case he blinked then said, "Second target down on the inside of the wall." The crackle of an assault rifle on full automatic ripped a hole in the morning. Lauren holstered her Glock, lying flat against the top of the wall, letting her legs swing down, dropping onto the sand next to the corpse, moving the Xiuhcoatl assault rifle from her shoulder to her hands.

Lane and Rodriguez had time to hit the ground before bullets ripped the bougainvillea. Ragged red petals and green leaves rained on them. Lane spat out a petal, checking to see if he was bleeding, returning fire, spattering the wall where he guessed the shooter was. When Lane stopped, Rodriguez fired a burst intent on keeping the shooter's head down.

Lane reached for a spare magazine, realizing the winner of this fight might be determined by who had the most ammunition.

Lauren said, "Three targets confirmed neutralized. I'll follow the wall. Work my way toward the fourth shooter." She heard two separate bursts and ducked.

Maria moved her drone along the wall, looking for the shooter, finding him between the wall and a mound of dirt. He was aiming at the centre of the garden where Maria knew Lane and Rodriguez were situated.

She heard a lull in the gunfire, seeing the shooter pulling a fresh clip from his bullet proof vest, sliding it into place, cocking his weapon, rolling to his left, the barrel of the gun pointing at her. Instinctively she ducked, hearing the chatter of automatic gunfire as the camera of her drone went grey. She looked across at Christine intent on the smartphone, sitting with her back against the wall of the house.

Maria reached for a second control, thumbing on the power, starting the third drone, hoping she would make it to her station before it was too late.

Christine squinted at her screen, seeing the shooter's muzzle flash, hearing the gunfire. She listened for the distinctive crackle of return fire from Lane and Rodriguez, wondering if Lauren would get to the shooter in time.

Christine flew her drone over the wall, out of sight of the

shooter.

She put her finger on the head of the shooter, lifted her index finger, making a swiping motion. The drone camera gave her a close-up as it skimmed the concrete, diving along the inside of the wall. The face of a man as he turned. The barrel of his weapon turning toward her. The expression on his face, a close up of his eyes. The drone camera went grey.

Lauren was on her belly, crawling along the wall. Bullets spattered the concrete above her, coating her with dust and debris. "Cease fire!" She waited before crawling forward, seeing the sole of one of the shooter's boots. "It's Lauren. I'm going to stand up. I'm near the shooter. Don't fucking shoot me!"

Lane said, "Understood."

She got to her knees, ready to hit the ground. She lifted one foot under her, weapon pointing at the shooter, seeing his chest rising, automatic rifle on the ground beside him. His right hand pulled the handgun from its holster. A glimpse of a face streaked with blood from a gash across the forehead, bone of the skull revealed. Her Xiuhcoatl assault rifle jerked once, twice, three times. The shooter took two at centre mass, one in the throat. He dropped his handgun, hands to his neck, blood pumping between his fingers.

Lauren kicked the handgun away before sticking the barrel of her weapon in his belly. "Shooter down. Angela! We need a medic!"

An emerald green hummingbird flew into a nearby bell-shaped purple blossom. Lauren was transfixed as the bird went from one blossom to the next before zipping away. The sound of its thrumming wings audible over the sound of Joe coughing blood.

Brenda Bruciarsi got up to answer the knock on her front door, taking a 50 from the counter as she passed, opening the door, handing the bill to the boy in the red shirt. The food was from Endeavour, a restaurant she had discovered last week. Their tortellini was a new favourite. She opened the bag, taking out the napkins and aluminum container. She had to use oven mitts to empty the dish onto her plate. She went to the table, sitting down, reaching for the chilled bottle of Beaujolais, pouring it into a glass, swirling the red, checking its legs before taking a sniff.

Her burner rang. "Shit!" She set the glass down, hoping the call was from KG. "Hello?"

"Any news from Mexico?"

She recognized Colin Wright's voice. "Not yet. He estimated today or tomorrow. I'll call you as soon as I hear." She hung up, setting the phone down, returning to the wine.

Outside and halfway down the block, the officer in the grey unmarked CPS van pressed a button on his phone. "Hashir? It's Ben. She just got a call asking about KG."

Hashir said, "Thanks. Forward the recording please."

Ben said, "Will do."

Nigel Li listened to the conversation between Bruciarsi and Wright Jr. "At least it proves a connection between them and the 45s. It should help with the totality of evidence."

Hashir nodded. "We'll keep at it."

"Anything more on Freddy Wright's killer?"

Hashir shook his head. "Not since the passport ID. The FBI is looking into it but it's probably an alias."

Nigel's smartphone chirped. He pulled it from his shirt

pocket, reading the message before turning it for Hashir to read. "It's from Lauren."

Thanks for the intel on the 45s. Attack came early this am. Four 45s involved. Two captured alive. Zero casualties on our side. Moving location. Will advise. L.

No one else wanted to drive KG's black Ram pickup with the two corpses wrapped in tarps in the back. Lane and Christine shrugged.

Lauren, Angela and Maria rode in the Expedition with KG in the back. They'd duct taped his mouth shut after he'd said, "I'm an American citizen. I have rights!" once too often.

The Suburban travelled in between the others. Petra drove, Andreas rode shotgun and Rodriguez kept a Glock on Rube who said nothing but kept popping his front teeth in and out until Petra said, "Listen pendejo, I'll tape your mouth if you don't shut it and keep it shut!"

The three vehicles travelled about fifty metres apart, heading for the military base in San Jose.

CHAPTER 12

Christine opened one eye. It had taken until three am for the adrenaline to flush itself from her system. She was hoping to sleep-in, maybe have a late breakfast before FaceTiming Dan and the kids, catching up with Alexandra about baby Karen.

A knock at her door. It was a low rent hotel with a single light bulb, non-functioning appliances, a shower with no curtain and a lovely manager named Maria who made every effort to make Christine feel at home.

Christine rolled out of bed, answering the door wearing a T-shirt and shorts, seeing Lauren who said, "Can you come with me? Veronica needs some help."

"Come in. Who's Veronica and where's my uncle?"

"Lane is with Rodriguez. They're interrogating the 45s. Okay if I explain about Veronica on the way?"

Lauren was sitting in a green plastic patio chair when Christine came out. Lauren pointed at the empty pond lined with blue, green and white tiles. "I want you to remember this pond. Do you know that in Palmilla–only a few kilometres from here–it's lush with vegetation because of all the water? Around here water means money and people like Maria can only afford so much of it." She led the way out the front gate where the Suburban was parked. "Climb in."

Lauren drove the Suburban along a dusty paved road bordered by houses, apartments and businesses.

Christine turned to Lauren. "Why are we talking about water? Is this some kind of delayed reaction after you had to kill that guy yesterday? It took a long time for my uncle to come to terms with shooting a guy to save a family."

Lauren shook her head. "I don't want to talk about that. We have work to do and I don't want to talk about it."

"He said much the same thing, internalized the experience, wondered if he was any different from the people he hunted. Then he finally came to the realization he did what had to be done. Just like you did what needed to be done."

"I don't fucking want to talk about it!"

"Okay. Have it your way. Who the fuck is this Veronica?"

"Her, Anna and I have been working with some other people."

Christine leaned against the seatbelt. "Anna as in Nigel and Anna?"

Lauren nodded. "Correct."

Christine's hands did the Flamenco as she said, "That's all very nonspecific. What other people?"

"You're kind of dangerous with the way–" Lauren used her index finger on the steering wheel pointing in Christine's direction– "you talk with your hands."

"Don't change the subject!"

Lauren laughed. "You are a piece of work."

"Deal with it!"

"Hell, I kinda like it!"

Nigel, Rhonda and Hashir drank coffee, sitting on either side of a round table, staring at the flat screen TV attached to the wall. Hashir pressed the remote. "A series of images from airport surveillance show Donald Colton boarding flights to

McCarran International Airport in Las Vegas, Nevada. There are other images from Calgary, Denver, New York, LA, Mexico City and Toronto. Each of these visits coincides with unsolved murders of people in some way connected with WTF, CNIG and/or the 45s." Hashir flipped thought the images.

Nigel leaned closer.

Rhonda said, "Slow down, please. I want to make sure it's the same guy in each image."

Hashir nodded, handing her the remote. "The final picture is a real find."

She stopped at the image of a man in a red robe, holding a Confederate battle flag and wearing a pointed red hat with the visor pulled up. "You have to be shitting me."

Nigel said, "It's the same guy."

Hashir nodded. "Grand Dragon Beauregard Logan."

Nigel said, "Pass it along to Lauren."

Lane sat alongside Rodriguez. The room was whitewashed concrete with metal chairs and table. The general wore a sparkling uniform. Lane wore borrowed military gear and aviator sunglasses.

Rodriguez said something in Spanish. And as agreed, Lane said, "General Rodriguez wants me to explain about FATF."

Rube wore an orange jumpsuit and hand cuffs attached to ankle chains. His front teeth had been removed for safekeeping; his shaved head dotted with sweat. He looked from Lane to Rodriguez and back again. "What's FATF?"

"The Financial Action Task Force." He pointed at Rodriguez then at himself. "We track the money used to finance terrorism."

"I'm no terrorist! I'm an American!" Rube tried to lift his hands but reached the end of his chain. "Shit! I want a lawyer!"

Lane pushed his glasses up the bridge of his nose with his

forefinger. "There are a different set of procedures for terrorists."

"I told you, I'm not a terrorist!"

Lane opened a folder. "These are photographs of the weapons, drugs and money found in the captured vehicles you travelled in." He stood, taking each of the six photographs, taping them to the wall behind. Then he wrote TERRORIST on another paper, taping it above the photos.

Rube said, "Are you fuckin' deaf? I'm not a terrorist. KG told us we were supposed to take care of some Mexicans who were kidnapping Americans! They're the terrorists!"

Lane sat down, reaching into a second folder, pulling out a photograph of a man in a red robe and conical cap. "This is Dalton Colton aka Joe. One of your comrades. He is a person of interest in a murder in Canada. He is a person of interest in several other unsolved murders. He is also known as Beauregard Logan, Grand Dragon in the Ku Klux Klan. Are you aware the KKK is a terrorist organization?"

"What?"

Lane scratched the top of his head. "This guy–" he pointed at the photo of the Grand Dragon "–is a member of a terrorist organization and you arrived in Todos Santos with a Glock handgun and a Colt assault rifle. You were in a vehicle with two kilos of cocaine, accompanied by Mr. Beaureguard Logan and Mr. Kush Gumbay-Yaw. Mr. Gumbay-Yaw is implicated in a series of terrorist operations inside and outside the US in his capacity as a member of a terrorist organization called the 45s."

"I'll tell you again. I'm not a terrorist. I'm an American citizen. I was told I was taking out kidnappers preying on American tourists."

Lane turned, looking at the photographs. "The evidence says otherwise." He turned back, seeing the perspiration rolling down the side of Rube's face and ever-expanding dark orange patches under his arms.

Rube lifted his chin. "You CIA?"

Lane shrugged.

"Homeland?"

Another shrug, this time with raised eyebrows.

Rube stuck his tongue in the gap of his front teeth then leaned back. "If we can make a deal, I'll tell you everything I know about KG and the 45s."

Lauren parked next to a gold taxi van. Its driver sat on a bench under the shade of a tree. Lauren left the engine running, air-conditioning pushing cold air. "You're a teacher."

Christine nodded, watching two tourists wobble out of a tequila shop.

"Veronica needs a proofreader. She worries about word choice in English."

"Why can't you check it?"

"I'm a detective, not a teacher. This piece she's writing, there's little room for error."

Christine studied Lauren. "When I ask you a question, you tell me you don't want to talk about it. Now you've got this job for me and you want me to take your word for it. You want me to trust you but on your terms. From my point of view, it smells of bullshit."

Lauren looked out the windshield. *I wonder how well she'll handle the truth?* "When I first met Lane it was during the Calgary floods. I had to look into Lane's background after the death of a psychopath who was in the Mexican government. Lane and Arthur set up a fund for schools and hospitals right here in San Jose. They found the account details of a heavy-duty drug cartel, emptied the accounts and got together with some locals to fund this community."

"I remember them talking – in pretty general terms – about something after they got back from a trip to Mexico."

"Anna found out about it too. She and I got talking at her place. Then we talked some more."

Christine opened her mouth then closed it. *Just listen.*

"She contacted Alejandro. He wasn't all that interested until we got Veronica and Rodriguez in on it."

"In on what?" Christine put a hand over the air-conditioning outlet.

"A crazy idea about making everyone, including the Untouchables, pay their fair share."

"Untouchables?"

"Wealthy Canadians. The Canada Revenue Agency made amnesty deals with Untouchables when it discovered they were hiding money in offshore accounts as a tax dodge."

"But we're here." Christine pointed out her window.

"It's not just some wealthy people in Canada. It's happening all over."

"So, you wanted to do something about it?"

Lauren lifted her eyebrows. "It's already been done." She pulled her phone from the pocket in her shorts. "Extractions were done simultaneously this morning."

"Extractions?"

"We took money from offshore Untouchable accounts."

Christine looked outside at a farmacia advertising ED drugs depicting Pancho in a sombrero with a toothy grin. *Holy shit! What the hell have I gotten myself into?*

Petra and Angela wore their combat uniforms, sitting across from KG in the room where Rube had been interrogated.

KG wore hand and ankle cuffs, orange coveralls and sandals. "You señoritas must be room service."

Petra opened the first file. "We have a signed confession implicating you in carrying out a series of murders in Mexico, the US and Canada."

KG shook his head. "You gonna tell me who took my boots? They're custom made. Cost more than you two make in a year."

Angela opened a second file, sliding out a picture of Grand Dragon Beauregard Logan. "This is your associate who was killed in Todos Santos yesterday. He was a member of a terrorist organization."

KG studied the photo, smiling. "I don't know that guy. We were hired to rescue two American children being held by kidnappers. My employer paid us to rescue the kids and return them to the U.S."

Petra pulled out another photograph of KG and Brenda Buciarsi meeting at a pool patio. "This photograph was taken last week in Tucson. This woman hired you to eliminate a threat to her investors."

KG shook his head. "I meet lots of people. It was a business meeting about investments."

Angela pushed a photograph of Chris Spicer in between Bruciarsi and Logan. "Mr. Spicer was a contractor from San Diego not a member of S.E.A.L. Team Six."

"That lyin' sack of shit!"

Petra said, "He broke his neck when he fell over the wall."

"You should be thanking me for helping you eliminate those two guys. I should get some kinda medal or amnesty because those two forced me into this."

Petra took photocopies from her file. "Your associate, Rupert MacIntyre – the one you call Rube – provided access to his bank account. It reveals a series of entries into his account. He confirmed he was paid by you to engage in other terrorist activities both in Mexico and the U.S."

"Those are fake. This whole thing is fake! I'm an American citizen kidnapped by terrorists and being held illegally!"

Angela leaned closer. "We are not interested in your fictional account of what happened. We found these photographs on your phone." She held it up. "It contains pictures of two Canadian citizens in the compound at the time of your attack. You were hired to eliminate them, not rescue them as you claim."

"That phone has a password! You've invaded my privacy!"

Petra stood. "Let's go."

Angela collected the folders. "We have the evidence required to charge you as a terrorist Mr. Gumbay-Yaw. You were hired to commit a terrorist act on Mexican soil and you worked with a known terrorist." She stood up, following Petra out the door.

"I'm not a terrorist! I'm an American!"

Christine and Lauren walked past the glass display case in the Riviera Nuevo Café located a block south of the San Jose cathedral. Christine turned when she heard the owner – a woman of thirty, wearing white with a red apron, a ready smile and wary eyes – lock the door behind them. They sat across the blue pearl granite table from Veronica who had a cup of coffee and her laptop.

Lauren said, "Veronica, this is Lane's niece Christine."

Christine said, "Mucho gusto."

Veronica smiled, waving Christine to sit next to her on the bench. "I need some help to make sure these are the right words in English. It is important this article be accurate."

Christine got up, sliding in next to Veronica who smelled of lavender. She read the top of the article. "What is FresaLeaks?"

Veronica said, "It is what you would call a non-profit organization providing information about social justice issues. This article is about money hidden by the super rich. How our revolution has begun."

Christine looked at Lauren. "Revolution?"

Lauren nodded. "For the last half century more and more of the world's wealth has been concentrated in the hands of a few. This article outlines how the revolution has begun and what it hopes to accomplish."

"Shit!"

Veronica said, "I believe the English word is bullshit." She pointed at Lauren and then at the woman in the red apron. "For many years we have grown tired of the bullshit." She pointed at her heart. "We decided something must be done."

Christine read the first line. "This revolution begins with 18.5 trillion dollars." She looked at all three women as a tray of coffees arrived and the owner sat across. "The opening line sure is catchy."

Lauren said, "This is Isa."

Christine nodded. "Mucho gusto." She sipped her coffee. "Perfecto."

Isa smiled, sipping her coffee, getting up, returning with croissants. "Comer."

Christine read, broke off a bit of croissant and made suggestions to Veronica who mostly agreed.

Near the end of the article and third croissant, Christine pointed at the screen. "How did you work out the amount of money to be removed from the accounts?"

Veronica tilted her head to one side, looking at the ceiling. "I calculated the number of days in the offshore account, worked in each nation's tax based on income, added in compound interest, then worked with Alejandro and Anna on the program."

Christine looked at Lauren.

Lauren said, "Veronica is a matemático and Alejandro a computer whiz. You already know Anna."

There was knock on the glass door. Isa got up, going to the door, locking it behind Alejandro who wore his work clothes.

He took off his hat. "It's already happening. The Thomaso family got a call from the father, from Elvis. They packed up and left after that. Mark told me they were told to fly to the Cayman Islands." Alejandro wiped at his eyes, Veronica stood, hugging him as his shoulders shook.

Veronica rubbed his back, turning her head. "Mark was Alejandro's little amigo."

Alejandro asked, "What have we done to this little boy?"

Petra and Angela sat down across from KG in the white interrogation room. Both women waited with unopened files on the table.

"Moby and Curtis Drayten," KG said.

Petra remained impassive.

"You wanted the names of the people who hired me to take out the contract on Freddy Wright." KG had his hands together, fingers intertwined.

Angela opened her file, writing the names on a sheet of lined paper. "Who are Moby and Curtis?"

"I first met them when I was playing football in high school. They were alumni and helped me get into college. They run Drayten Industries. It's a mining, oil and construction company."

Petra yawned.

"They are the guys behind CNIG and WTF."

Petra said, "Those are Canadian companies."

KG laughed. "That's what everyone is supposed to think. The Drayten's are smart. They keep a low profile. They tell me that a whale never gets harpooned if it stays below the surface. That's what they do. They stay under the surface. They get people like me and Brenda to do their dirty work for them."

Petra asked, "Brenda?"

KG nodded, getting into the telling of his story, sensing his audience was receptive. "Brenda Bruciarsi. Used to work for the Prime Minister up in Canada. Was a fixer for him, now she works as a fixer for WTF and CNIG. They think she's working for them. I think it's the other way around. You think I didn't check her out with the Drayten's? I'm a smart guy!"

Petra tapped the table with her forefinger. "You're here."

KG's pupils narrowed as he stared at Petra. "We both know

I won't be here for very long."

Angela said, "Oh, that's right. You haven't seen the news."

KG asked, "What news?"

FRESALEAKS
Creating a more just society in the Americas
The Untouchables Pay

By V

The Catrina Revolution began with 18. 5 trillion dollars being removed from the offshore accounts of Untouchables. It happened early this morning.

We have known about some of the world's wealthiest (often referred to as one percenters) illegally transferring money into offshore accounts. Governments have known it as well and have either been complicit, unwilling, or unable to address the problem.

Today marks a change in this policy of having one small group of untouchable individuals amassing massive wealth on the backs of impoverished millions.

In no way does The Revolution punish the prosperous few who share their wealth in a variety of ways with contributions to charities and initiatives aimed at improving the lives of others.

The Catrina Revolution is a realignment of wealth, aimed at those who seek to avoid paying their share. The money owed in taxes, with interest compounded, will now be used to improve the lives, health, and education of people who have so often been exploited by a group of extremely wealthy individuals.

Information on the specific amounts removed from individual and corporate accounts can be found on our web page: www.fresaleaks.com

For further updates on the revolution follow Catrina on YouTube.

Alexandra wondered why no one ever told her how painful breastfeeding could be as she stroked Karen's cheek. The pair had worked into a bit of a routine. Matt prepared supper. Indy and Ella played outside while Rory kept a lookout. Alexandra and Karen would sit, snuggle and bond in the easy chair. Alexandra caught up on the news while her daughter fed. She reached for the TV remote with her free hand, turning up the volume, listening, glancing at Karen as she turned toward the sound. "Matt, you might want to see this."

Matt came into the living room with a tea towel tucked into his shorts. "What?"

"They're showing pictures of the Grand Bahama and Owen Roberts International Airports."

"Owen Roberts?"

"In the Cayman Islands."

Karen broke suction. Alexandra pressed mute on the remote. Karen latched back on. Alexandra pointed at the TV.

"Private jets have been arriving," she said, lifting her chin. "I think that's a picture of the Isle of Man Airport. I was there once on a business trip."

Matt looked over his shoulder, seeing Rory keeping an eye on the kids in the backyard.

"What's going on?"

"They are running out of places to park the private jets." She pointed at the screen where aircraft parked on the grass at the edges of taxiways. Another shot showed concrete aprons jammed with jets parked in an aero jigsaw puzzle. "They say it's unprecedented and something to do with this FresaLeaks thing where money was taken from the accounts of some of the super-rich. It's crazy."

"Did you say FresaLeaks?"

"Yes."

Matt sat on the arm of the chair. "The kids at school were talking about some kind of revolution that's going viral. Something about trillions of dollars taken from overseas bank accounts."

"You're kidding." Alexandra looked at the TV and images of the airport crowded with all manner of private planes. One was a white wide body jet with no visible markings.

"Do you remember Arthur talking about something he and Lane worked on in Cabo? They found drug money and used it to fund schools and hospitals?"

Matt took a breath, pulling out his phone. "Shit! Christine texted me and said she thought maybe Anna was a member of FresaLeaks. Do you think?"

Alexandra stroked Karen's cheek, then looked up at Matt. "I think maybe the kids better come inside. And I think we need to FaceTime with Christine."

"Wait a minute." Matt reached for the remote. "That's the reporter Collette Janjua. She's usually got something interesting to say.

"Don't wake Karen up."

INN NEWS

(INT- Studio news set - A white haired woman wearing a grey suit, pink shirt and blue tie stands behind a round glass table. She is framed by TVs on either side of her. Both show a white, wide-bodied airliner surrounded by smaller private jets.)

"This is Collette Janjua for INN News. We are looking at Owen Roberts International Airport. Grand Cayman's main airport. I've been there several times, and can say from firsthand experience that what we are seeing is very unusual. We have just confirmed that the white unmarked Boeing 777, nicknamed Moby Dick, belongs to Moby Drayten. He and his brother Curtis are often referred to as the richest family in

America.

"The Drayten jet, along with the many others at the airport, appears to be part of a disorganized exodus of some of the wealthiest people in North America, Europe and Asia.

"At this time we have been unable to confirm the reasons for the exodus. The Grand Cayman Airport was closed to incoming traffic as of an hour ago. We are attempting to get a reporter on the ground at Owen Roberts as we speak.

"We'll keep you updated as further information becomes available. Please stay tuned to INN News."

The newscast cut to a commercial and Matt pressed mute. "Supper's almost done."

Alexandra asked, "Does this have anything to do with Christine and Paul?"

He went to the back door, opening it. "Supper guys!"

Nigel knocked for the fourth time on the door of Bruciarsi's third floor condo. The grey carpet smelled of cleaning solution. He heard Hashir breathing, his phone vibrating.

Hashir reached in his jacket pocket, reading a text. "The uniforms are checking the security video to see if she snuck out."

Nigel knocked again, listening for sounds of activity. "Can you track her phone?"

Dan's tablet played a tango. He tapped its face, smiling at the image of Christine who sat in front of a cream-coloured wall.

Alexandra asked, "Is that her?" She appeared next to Dan.

Christine asked, "How are the kids? How is Karen?"

"Good. Gaining weight. Loving the boob." Alexandra became the middle of the sandwich when Matt arrived.

Christine said, "I miss you guys."

Matt asked, "Where are you?"

Christine looked left and right. "In a room."

Alexandra said, "No shit Sherlock."

Dan asked, "Paul okay?"

Christine nodded. "We've been moving around a bit. He seems better. He was pretty pissed when I first got here. I think he's over it now."

Alexandra said, "We read FresaLeaks."

"How did you know about that?" Christine leaned out of the camera then returned. "Can we talk more when I get home? I have to go. Love you. Hug the kids for me."

The FaceTime connection ended.

CHAPTER 13

Christine woke to the fat side of a fist pounding her door. "What?"

"It's Lauren. Get up! We need you again."

She rolled over, planting her feet on the floor. "What is it this time?"

"Anna can't be here – obviously – and she wants you to stand in for her. She says we need five. Something about a hand and the number of digits. Anyway, we have to get our makeup done. We're on in two hours. We gotta move."

INN Anchor, Collette Janjua, wears a blue jacket and slacks. The look is complemented with a red scarf.

She turns left to face a TV screen where five women sit side by side. Each has a white face with dark circles around the eyes, black makeup on noses and chins. All have skeletal mouths.

Apart from that, each is unique with hats ranging from fedora to beret. Flowers and bright-coloured accents also add to the individual aspects of each female face. All wear black T-shirts, uniting the Catrina imagery.

"Hello, I'm Collette Janjua and this is INN News Live. The International News Network has the first English language interview with five women claiming to have information about the transfer of wealth from offshore accounts resulting in an exodus of some of the richest families on three continents. Ladies, is there some significance to the makeup you're all wearing?"

Angela says, "We are Catrinas. If you are familiar with Mexican culture, you will understand the significance of what we wear. For those who are unfamiliar – in the most basic sense – Catrinas represent the equality of all people no matter their position in society."

"I understand not all of you are from Mexico."

"Two of us are Canadians."

Janjua asks, "You are connected with what is being called called the Catrina Revolution?"

All five Catrinas nod.

"We are," Angela says. "It has been many years in the planning. We decided to do something about the illegal concentration of wealth in the hands of people who are unwilling to contribute to the communities they exploit."

"Some are calling it theft."

Angela nods, "Yes, the theft has been going on for more than 50 years. We decided it was time to stop being victims and fight back."

"I meant, some are calling you thieves."

"I expect we will be called many things in the days to come. The wealth we took back has been placed in a not-for-profit Virtual Bank, which will contribute to the health, education and economic stability of North American men, women and children who have been marginalized."

"Lawyers representing Moby and Curtis Drayten say their clients are the victims here; that the Catrinas are thieves."

The women look at one another. The Catrina with red flowers in her hair begins to laugh. The others join in.

Janjua says, "Will you let us in on the joke?"

Christine, wearing beret and red beads outlining the black around her eyes, says, "The Draytens hired four men to kill us. Now they are acting like the victims. That's why it's funny."

"Do you have proof they hired men to kill you?"

Angela nods, "We sent you the picture of Beauregard Logan, Grand Dragon on the KKK. Do you have it here?"

An image of Logan in his red cape and hat appears on the screen.

"He died in the attack. Two of the four men survived. One has testified they were hired by the Draytens. We have checked his bank records and they confirm his story."

Janjua says, "How did Logan die?"

"We took him out and captured the other two when they arrived to kill us."

"That makes three. You said there were four."

Angela continues, "The fourth man fell off a wall and broke his neck. He was carrying a light machine gun while the others were armed with assault rifles. Cocaine and other weapons were found in their vehicles. We have video of it. A Canadian named Brenda Bruciarsi hired them. You recall she worked for the former Canadian Prime Minister? We have discovered this Bruciarsi was working for Wright Trust Financial and Canadian National Investors Group, whose ownership traces to the Drayten brothers."

"This is beginning to sound like a very complicated case. What brought five women together to take it on?"

Angela says, "We are just a few of the people involved. Each one of us has her own reasons. For me it was when Trump said he could grab women by la concha and then was elected President of the United States. That was a turning point for me."

Petra has red flowers in her hair and says, "I did not want to be a victim."

Maria, wearing a fedora, says, "I want my nieces and nephews to have a better future."

Lauren, wearing a camouflaged cadet cap, says, "The

Untouchables think they are above the law."

Christine, fiddling with her beret, says, "The pendejos were trying to kill my uncle."

The Catrinas laugh.

Petra says, "Your Spanish is improving!"

"Thank you Collette," says Angela. "If you would like to speak with us again, you know how to get in touch."

"And that is how the interview ended. I'm certain this is not the last we will hear of the Catrinas and their Revolution. For INN News, I'm Collette Janjua, in Calgary."

Barrett Duval's office was situated just west of Calgary International Airport in a brick and white-windowed building called Duval Developments. Nigel and Hashir walked up to the receptionist sitting behind a glass command centre. She was in her mid-twenties, blonde and blue-eyed, wearing a purple dress and black stilettos. Nigel estimated her shoes cost just under $1,000.

She asked, "You have an appointment?"

Nigel had his badge at the ready, opening it, holding it against the glass so she could read it. "No, no appointment. We understand Mr. Duvall is in his office."

She tapped the microphone at her cheek. "I'll ask. Please have a seat."

Hashir shook his head. "No thank you. Which way is his office?"

The receptionist glanced at the yellow metal steps leading to the second floor.

"Please let him know we are on our way." Nigel made for the staircase, his shoes singing on metal.

The wide-planked wood on the second floor was recycled oak. Hashir tapped Nigel on the shoulder, pointing at a corner office with the stylized letters of Duvall's name sandblasted into glass. Through the closed door, they could see a red-haired man on the phone talking, his eyes on the detectives. He wore a blue suit, red tie and white shirt. He stood.

Nigel knocked and opened the door. "Barrett Duvall?"

Duvall nodded. He was five foot eight, weighing maybe 180 pounds, sweat glistening on his forehead. Duvall remained behind the desk. "What's your pleasure gentlemen?"

Nigel waited for Hashir to stand next to him. Hashir pulled a phone from his pocket.

Duvall asked, "Can I see your ID?"

Nigel opened his ID. Hashir did the same, waiting for Duvall to read.

Nigel set a manila folder on the table. "We're here to ask you about Brenda Bruciarsi."

Duvall frowned. "Brenda who?"

Hashir took out his phone, setting it on the desk, pressing record. "You don't mind if I record this do you?"

Duvall looked out beyond them and the glass. "Uh, no."

"Were calls made from this office to Brenda Bruciarsi and did this office receive calls from Ms. Bruciarsi?"

"Not from me." Duvall smiled with whitened teeth.

Nigel opened his file and tapped a sheet of paper. "A Samsung phone in your name received and initiated calls to Bruciarsi."

Duvall shook his head. "I often leave my phone on my desk. Someone else must have used it."

Nigel said, "In your role as a member of the Police Commission have you used your influence to determine the location of CPS detective Lauren Jackson?"

Duvall's face was red. "Why aren't you guys tracking down the people who stole money from all those banks?"

Nigel pulled out a second sheet of paper. "We have a transcript of a call made from this office to Bruciarsi. Would you like to read it?" He then reached into his inside jacket pocket, bringing out his phone.

"You haven't answered my question! Have you caught the

people responsible for stealing trillions? Two of them are Canadians! Did you know that?"

Nigel tapped the face of his phone. "This is a recording of the call made from your Samsung phone. Do you recognize the voice?"

Nigel pressed play. He watched Duvall put his hand over his mouth. A recorded voice asked, "Have you received any news about my federal nomination?" Nigel turned to Hashir.

Hashir said, "Choose your next words very carefully Mr. Duvall. The recording is proof you used your influence to obtain information on the location of a CPS detective. That information was used to make an attempt on her life, the lives of five Mexican nationals and two Canadians."

Hashir tapped the table next to his phone. "We have a recording of you lying to us. Your political career is most likely over. Your business career–" He looked around the office, the plaques on the wall, the family pictures, the picture of Duvall golfing with Bill Shyne "–is hanging in the balance. Have you heard that Mr. Shyne attempted to leave the country yesterday and was arrested?"

Duvall nodded.

Nigel said, "My advice is that you retain a lawyer. If Bruciarsi manages to leave the country, we will be looking at adding to the charges against you." He picked up his folder and phone, setting his business card on the desk. "I estimate you have an hour. It would be best if you and your lawyer–" he tapped the business card "–arrive at our building with information on the location of Bruciarsi. The opportunity for negotiation is dependent on our locating and arresting her." He waited, following Hashir as they left the office, descending the yellow stairs, passing the receptionist, leaving by the front door.

A thunderstorm dumped a bellyful of rain on the roof.

Alexandra had to reach for the remote to adjust the volume so she could hear the TV. Ella cuddled next to her; Indy played a game on his iPod. Karen slept in her bassinet upstairs.

Ella said, "I miss my Mom."

Alexandra put her arm around Ella, adjusting to never having a moment to herself. "Me too. She'll be home soon." She watched as five women were being interviewed on INN.

Ella pointed. "Catrinas."

"How did you know that?"

"My teacher."

Alexandra tucked a strand of Ella's hair behind her ear while listening to the interview.

Indy didn't lift his head when he asked, "Why's my Mom on TV?"

Alexandra stood, picking Ella up, moving closer to the TV.

Ella said, "Mom swore."

Indy laughed.

Alexandra reached for the phone.

Angela sat behind the wheel of the Suburban. They'd stopped outside Christine's hotel where a dog of mixed parentage patrolled the rooftop. Eight of the Suburban's occupants inhaled as Christine climbed in, getting cheek to cheek. The air conditioning worked full time and everyone perspired.

Christine asked, "Where are we off to?"

Lane looked at Rodriguez who said, "We have been ordered back to Mexico City with the Americans." He pointed at Christine, Lauren and Lane. "You have been ordered to return to Canada."

Christine's eyebrows made two creases across her forehead. "Ordered?" She looked around at the people in the Suburban. "What about Veronica and Alejandro?"

Andreas turned around in the front passenger seat. "They

are on their way to Leona Vicario near Cancun."

Angela tapped Christine on the shoulder. "It will be alright. We have planned for this. We never expected these rich and powerful people–whose lives are centred around their wealth–to allow us to walk away without a fight."

Lauren tapped a knuckle against her window. "Ottawa sent a plane to pick us up." She looked out at the dusty streets and bougainvillea, wondering if she'd ever be able to come back.

Christine asked, "You okay, Lauren?"

She smiled. "Just drinking it all in. I like it here." She looked at the faces of the women and men around her. "I've never been in combat before. It's hard to explain."

Angela said, "We won't forget what you did."

Rodriguez said, "I was hoping I could repay my debt to Paul and now I have a debt to you. It could have gone either way with the killer until you–" he pointed at Christine and then Lauren "–did what was necessary." He tapped Lane on the shoulder. "It appears your country has women as fierce as our adelitas."

Christine asked, "What happens to the two Americans?"

Petra said, "They are on their way to Mexico City to be interviewed." She glanced at Maria who lifted her chin.

Christine frowned. "What?"

Maria smiled. "Politicians want to have their pictures taken with the terrorists from the US. It will be a telenovela. Dramatic pictures with American terrorists, weapons and drugs."

Andreas said, "It will make great TV. Just not as good as five Catrinas!"

Laughter filled the cabin, lightening the mood, leading to string of jokes, taking them the rest of the way to the San Jose airport.

Anna sat under an umbrella at a table outside The Café with

Natalie who decided to share her mom's pancakes. Her fingers were sticky with syrup migrating to her hair. The black curls were stuck together, forming stringy bangs. She swiped her hair back, making a sticky situation stickier.

Louise arrived with a carafe of coffee and a second plate of pancakes. "Need a refill?"

Anna reached into the bag under Natalie's stroller, pulling out a manila envelope. "I almost forgot to give you this. It's an application for a bursary from International Virtual Bank. Just fill it out and give it back to me. My phone number is in there. Did you look at the culinary arts program?"

Louise set the carafe down. Her eyes began to fill with tears. "Why are you doing this?"

Natalie looked up, pancake dough on her cheeks, sensing the tension, turning to her mother.

"Do you want to sit down for a minute?"

Louise looked over her shoulder at the tables inside.

Anna said, "It's not very busy. Can you take a minute?"

Louise sat. "Sometimes I think if I sit down, I won't be able to get back up."

"I'm gonna talk with your boss and get you a cup. You like coffee don't you?"

Louise smiled. The tears started again. She watched Natalie massacre her pancakes while Anna got up, going inside, returning with a second cup. "Gloria said it's fine if you take a break."

Louise nodded as Anna poured her a cup, then sat down across from her. Anna said, "My kid loves the pancakes as much as I do." She pulled out some wipes, ready to clean Natalie's face and was greeted with a 'don't mess with me while I'm eating look' stopping her halfway. "You asked why and it's because you do so much for your kids. You always talk about them. You worry about their future. You want better for them. I understand that. And I would like to help you and your kids." She tapped the white envelope. "Do you like the coffee here?"

Louise lifted the cup. "Love it actually." She took a sip. "I…

Thank you. I'm scared, I guess. I got used to working like this. Even the possibility of being able to go back to school, I thought it was out of the question and now…" She set the cup down. Anna handed her the baby wipes and Louise blew her nose.

Anna's phone rang. She read the number, looking at Louise who went to get up. "Please wait." Anna picked up the phone. "Hey Alexandra, what's new?"

"What the fuck is my sister doing on TV dressed up like a fucking skeleton!"

Anna looked at Louise whose eyes and mouth were open wide.

Anna said, "So you recognized her?"

"Indy did! Well? What's going on?"

"They're on their way home. I'm pretty sure it'll be okay. She should be back in a day or two."

Alexandra asked, "WHAT THE FUCK IS GOING ON?"

Natalie held up a morsel of pancake, smiled and said, "Fuck."

Louise chuckled.

Anna said to Alexandra, "Can you guess what my daughter's new word is?"

The white Government of Canada Challenger jet had a maple leaf painted on its nose. It was parked outside a building north of the main terminals at Los Cabos International Airport. Lauren, Christine and Lane hauled their luggage up to the jet's open door. A soldier waited at the steps as they approached. She wore green fatigues, a black beret and boots. There was a Canadian flag on her shoulder. Her name tag said 'Murdoch.' "Passports?"

Lauren reached inside her shoulder bag. Lane into his shirt pocket. Christine had hers at the ready.

Lauren asked, "Where are my pills?"

Lane said, "Can we try it without the pills?"

Lauren shook her head.

Murdoch held each passport up, comparing the pictures to their faces before handing them back. "Leave the luggage with me. I'll stow it."

Christine wondered how Murdoch had made a perfect circle with the brown bun of hair at the back of her head.

Lane waited for Lauren who waited for Christine. It was a short-lived Canadian comedy.

They all kept their heads down until finding three seats over the wing. A man in civilian clothes–white open-neck shirt, blue jeans and red cross trainers–sat at the back intent on his laptop. They waited as Murdoch stowed their bags, closing the door, moving to the cockpit. "Ready to depart."

Lane turned to Lauren. "You're into yoga right?"

Lauren nodded.

He said, "Concentrate on the breathing."

She closed her eyes, taking long breaths.

Christine's phone chirped. She reached for her purse, pulling out her phone, reading a text, tapping out a reply.

Murdoch stood over Christine, holding out her hand. "Phone."

Christine leaned away. "No thank you. My sister has some questions."

"Phone!" Murdoch put her hand on Christine's shoulder.

Christine looked over her shoulder. "Back off!"

Lane stood.

Lauren pushed herself up.

The guy at the back of the plane closed his laptop. "I'm Enrique. My friends call me Quique. We need your phones only for a moment to ensure they are not bugged. They will be returned. It is for your safety and ours. We would prefer not to be tracked. We are not going to Ottawa as you were told initially."

Lauren asked, "Where are we going then?"

Quique stood. "I can check the phones while the pilots do their run-up if you like, then I will tell you. It would be best if no-one has any idea where we are headed. After the attack in Todos Santos, precautions are required. Agreed?" He looked at Lane. "I could check yours first, so Christine has time to text Alexandra."

Lauren said, "You certainly are well informed."

Quique shrugged. "It's my job."

Lane handed his phone over, so did Lauren. Quique went back to his seat, checking the phones while Christine texted.

Lane asked, "Everything okay with Alexandra and the kids?"

Christine's thumbs danced across the keyboard. "She was watching TV with the kids. Indy and Ella recognized me. Alexandra wants to know what the fuck is going on. Her words."

Lauren kept her eyes closed, inhaling, exhaling. "You have smart kids. No-one from my family noticed anything about the Catrinas."

"Too smart sometimes." Christine finished texting, handing the phone to a hovering Murdoch. Then she turned, looking over her shoulder. "So, where are we headed?"

Quique took Christine's phone from Murdoch without looking up. "Cold Lake. Heard of it?"

The first engine began to wind up.

Barrett Duvall's lawyer was 50-plus, with perfectly trimmed silver hair, a double chin, grey suit and pink shirt. The frames of his designer glasses were a singular scarlet hue. He sat next to his client and across from Hashir, Nigel and Crown Prosecutor Rohan Misra. He wore a herringbone jacket with oversized brown buttons, a sharply defined beard and a toothy smile.

The conference room door was closed. Duvall's lawyer spoke first. "I am Roland Dixon, Mr. Duvall's solicitor. I understand you have some concerns about the behaviour of one of my client's business associates?"

Nigel waited.

Rohan asked, "Why don't we cut the bullshit?" He pointed at Dixon who attempted a smile and failed. "I've looked at the evidence. Your client's political career is over. If this goes to trial, it will stick to you like shit on a blanket. And it's a safe bet the business will take a big hit. We have the additional bonus of Mr. Duvall being an accessory to attempted murder."

Hashir's phone chirped. He read the text, showing it to Nigel under the table.

Rohan leaned over, reading the text. "Time to shit or get off the pot Barrett."

Dixon held his hand out. "It's just a ploy. You've got nothing."

Barrett said, "I have her phone number."

Nigel stood. "So do we."

"Not this one you don't." Barrett Duvall reached into his pants pocket pulling out his phone. "Take a look."

Hashir wrote the number down on his phone before forwarding it to Rhonda.

Lane observed the gradual change from a parched landscape where green was the result of irrigation, to a proliferation of sloughs, lakes, rivers and dugouts. It was as if crossing the border into Canada turned the tap on, changing the landscape from withered to lush.

Buildings, roads, bridges came into view in the west. A river snaked its way through the city centre as his ears popped from the loss in altitude. He spotted the domes of a sandstone building. *No way this is Cold Lake.* Lane looked left at Lauren then to the back of the aircraft where Quique was focused on his laptop. Murdoch's perfect bun was visible up front. Lane looked back at Lauren, lifting his chin, catching her eye, mouthing the word, "Edmonton."

Lauren nodded, passing on the message to Christine who glanced at Lane, lifting her chin in reply.

Nigel turned when Hashir walked into his office. "What's the latest on Bruciarsi? Any luck with her location?"

Hashir sat down across from Nigel. "I've got an unconfirmed report she's at Canadian Forces Base Edmonton."

"You're kidding me?"

"Rhonda has been on the phone for the last 30 minutes trying to find out what's going on and getting the runaround."

"Did she try EPS and the RCMP?"

Hashir nodded.

"How about CSIS?"

Hashir said, "Yes, she tried them all."

"They're not at liberty to discuss?"

"More or less."

Nigel stood. "Let me see what I can do. Bruciarsi is a person of interest in a murder investigation. No way we're gonna lose her because she's in the middle of some bureaucratic tangle." His phone chirped. He picked it up, reading a text, then frowning.

"Everything okay?"

"My wife and daughter are in Edmonton." Nigel looked out the open door then at Hashir. His phone chirped again. Nigel read the text message, shaking his head, turning the phone for Hashir to see.

Hashir asked, "Who is Keely Saliba and what does she know about Bruciarsi?"

Nigel tapped WTF on his phone, sending the text.

Keely Saliba's shoulder length red hair was tied back. There were streaks of untouched grey. She stood up, arching her back. She wore a navy-blue jacket, white blouse, military boots and red pants with a stretchy panel out front.

Anna stood near the wall as the hangar door opened, revealing the nose of a Challenger jet with its engines spooling down. "Natalie! Come here!"

Natalie looked over her shoulder. Her legs propelled the strider bike across the polished concrete floor. She wore an electric green helmet with yellow spikes.

Keely's phone chirped. She read the message while Anna herded Natalie close to the back wall. Keely held up her phone, lifting her chin to Anna. "I have a message from your husband."

Anna pulled Natalie and her bike over, reading the message. "Short and to the point as always."

"How much does he know?"

Anna lifted one eyebrow, dropping the other. "I kind of thought the less he knows the better."

"He's gonna be pissed?"

Anna smiled. "Oh yeah."

They watched as Lauren, Christine and Lane stepped through the Challenger's door and onto the concrete. Lane's head lifted. He spotted Natalie first then Anna and Keely. He stopped, eyes narrowing, head tilting to one side before moving toward them, hugging them in turn. "I've got a few of the details. How long have you been planning this?"

Lauren said, "A while."

Keely lifted her eyebrows. "Okay if we sit down? This one is doing somersaults." She patted her belly, looking at Lane. "Due in a month since you're asking." She turned, walking toward the back of the hangar where a plastic crate was next to a hallway leading to the washrooms and office. She sat. "That's better."

Lane looked around. Natalie resumed riding her strider bike in circles then figure eights. "Who are we waiting for?"

Keely stood. "I need to pee–" she pointed at Lane "–and coffee is on its way." She walked down the hallway, saying over her shoulder, "Politicians and an elder. That's who we're waiting for."

Christine followed Keely down the hallway. "How come we ended up in Edmonton instead of Cold Lake?"

Keely said, "The elder is here."

Lauren stood alongside Lane and Anna, watching Natalie. "We kept everyone else in the dark for as long as possible to minimize opportunities for leaks and for their own protection."

Lane nodded. "You two and Keely are the ring leaders?"

Anna smiled. "Lauren and I met when she was investigating you after the floods. We started talking. I told her about what you, Arthur and the others accomplished in San Jose. Over time we got talking about the Untouchables, then we brought Keely in. Lauren met her at a conference in Winnipeg. That's when we began to see all of the different pieces and how it would all have to work."

Lane looked around; eyes wide.

Lauren patted him on the back. "Rodriguez said we needed to bring you in because of your insights and instincts."

Anna touched his elbow. "Rodriguez was pretty sure there would be complications and you would be able to adapt."

Lane lifted his eyebrows. "I haven't been at my best lately."

Lauren kept her eyes on Natalie. "We need you if and when shit goes sideways."

Anna lifted her chin. "What's this?"

All three turned as two green SUVs pulled up, parking on the concrete outside the open hangar door. Six men in black short-sleeved shirts, bullet proof vests, black pants, boots and red berets lined up in front of the SUVs. A seventh man stood behind them wearing a blue uniform and red beret. He walked between the men in black. "I am Colonel Russell. You are being arrested under orders from the Minister of National Defence."

Natalie looked over her shoulder, gliding her bike, stopping next to her mother.

Lane asked, "Do you have written orders?"

If it was possible to stand straighter, that's what the colonel did before placing his fists on his hips. "Of course."

Lane held his hand out. "Let's see them."

Lauren turned to Anna. "Keep Natalie close."

Christine and Keely walked up the hallway. Christine said, "Giving birth is a lot like taking a big shit." She spotted the MPs. "What the hell is going on?"

Keely pulled her ID from the side pocket of her purse. "I'm with the RCMP."

Murdoch poked her head out the door of the jet. "I've been ordered to guard these civilians and hand them over to Singh."

Colonel Russell tapped the flashes on his shoulders. "You will do as ordered."

Murdoch looked confused.

Russell and his men moved closer. "We will call social services. The child will be well cared for."

Lauren, Lane, Christine and Keely moved up between the military police and Natalie who was picked up by Anna with one arm while pulling her phone from her pocket, using her thumb. "This is being recorded and transmitted."

The colonel stopped, his men doing the same.

Murdoch made up her mind, moving to stand next to Lauren. "As I said, they are my responsibility."

Lane said, "And we haven't seen your copy of the orders."

A green panel van pulled up followed by a red minivan. The corporal driving the panel van opened his window. "Somebody ordered food?"

Lane looked past the colonel and his men, raising his hand. "And some coffee?"

Christine giggled.

He turned to her, whispering. "Follow my lead." He waved at the corporal. "Can you bring the van inside and park it here?" He pointed at the middle of the hangar floor.

The corporal said, "No problem." He maneuvered his van in between the opposing sides, stopping, moving to the back of the van, opening the rear doors.

A woman in her 60s opened the driver's door of the red van, stepping out, hefting a multi-coloured knitted bag. The woman wore jeans, tennis shoes and a red cowboy shirt with white piping. Her black braided hair touched the backs of her knees.

The colonel looked around, noticing he was losing the logistical advantage, turning to the woman. "What the hell are you doing here?"

The woman in the red shirt walked around the back of the van, opening the hatch, pointing at one of the military police dressed in black. "Name is Tammy Crowchild. Please give me a hand with the table?" Her voice was a combination of soft almost musical tones and self-assurance. Everyone in the hangar had to be quiet to hear.

The brown-eyed and black-haired military police officer did as he was asked, lifting the table from the back of the van, following the woman in the red shirt, unfolding the legs of the small wooden table, setting it on its feet. Tammy said, "And the wooden box, please." The MP nodded, setting a handmade, wooden box on the table.

Colonel Russell said, "Crowshoe! Back in line!"

Crowshoe did as ordered.

Russell said, "I've been ordered to arrest them. Social Services will ensure the child's safety."

Tammy frowned, eyes narrowing. Lauren recognized profound sadness and anger in the expression. Tammy said, "The child appears to want to stay with its mother. Children are capable of knowing who they want to be with. The Minister of National Defence, Manpreet Singh, is coming to this meeting. We will wait for her and the others."

"Others?" Russell blushed.

Tammy nodded. "That coffee smells good." She looked at Lauren and Christine. "Anyone else feel like a coffee?"

The corporal said, "And sandwiches."

Tammy smiled at the corporal. "That would be very nice. Thank you."

Lauren looked, sensing how Tammy had changed the atmosphere inside the hangar. Tammy turned to Anna. "What kind of sandwich would your daughter like?"

Natalie said, "Peanut butter and jam, please."

Tammy smiled, turning to the corporal. The corporal opened up a plastic container. "Coming up."

Tammy turned to Russell. "Truce?"

His phone rang, offering him time to consider the option. He pulled the phone from his breast pocket, holding a forefinger up. "I need to take this." He turned to walk out the hangar door.

Tammy nodded. "You will not move."

Russell looked from left to right, pressing answer. Everyone in the hangar heard the voice on the phone. "Russell! You there? They under arrest yet?"

Colonel Russell said, "I have them in sight."

Anna lifted her eyebrows. Lauren watched Tammy move toward the colonel, holding out her hand. He handed the phone over.

The voice at the other end said, "Russell, you fucking pussy! Are they under arrest or not? I've still got your superior on speed dial!"

Tammy said, "Hello, former Prime Minister Ross. Are you calling from somewhere in the Caribbean, or perhaps the Cayman Islands?"

"What? What the fuck are you doing on the phone?"

Tammy asked, "Where are you?"

"None of your fucking business."

Tammy said, "We are in the middle of negotiations over sandwiches and coffee. Please respect our privacy." She pressed end on the phone, looking at the colonel whose face was maple leaf red. "Please turn the phone off. It will interfere with our negotiations." She handed the phone back to him. Russell did as he was told. She asked, "Truce?"

Russell avoided eye contact with his subordinates, instead looked at Natalie as he said, "Truce."

Tammy said, "In that case, please put the weapons in the vehicle."

"Without looking at their commanding officer, six MPs walked to the SUVs, opening the back hatches, ejecting the clips from their sidearms, checking the chambers, setting the weapons inside. They returned to Tammy, silently waiting on the colonel.

Natalie ate the middle of a peanut butter and jam sandwich, eyes on the soldiers.

Thirty-seven minutes later, more than a dozen people had eaten, been caffeinated or watered and had scrounged enough chairs so all could sit while leaving enough vacant for expected guests.

Lauren, Lane, Christine, Anna, Natalie and Murdoch remained huddled together, keeping Natalie within arm's reach. Keely and Tammy returned from a visit to the washroom. Tammy pointed at two large sedans pulling up. "How 'bout we get started? Anyone got any complaints about sitting man, woman, man, woman while Natalie rides her bike?"

Crowshoe asked, "What do you want us to do?" He raised his hand, pointing at his comrades.

Tammy said, "Sit. Every voice will be heard." She turned to the slender, grey-haired man with the designer glasses, the only person wearing a suit and tie. "This is Robert MacWhirter, Minister of Finance. Since there are significant financial implications, the Prime Minister requested he be here, along with Minister of Foreign Affairs, Nathan Chu." She indicated a short dark-haired man with long limbs, an athlete's grace, wearing sweatpants and a T-shirt. "Over here we have Manpreet Singh, Minister of Defence representing the armed forces." Manpreet wore a black turban, sleeveless red top and black slacks. She watched Natalie weaving in and out of the chairs, using the meeting as a complex obstacle course. "And our honoured guest and cyclist is Natalie, who is Anna's daughter." Tammy stood, making her way to the table. "Her safety and access to her mother are guaranteed."

Russell asked, "Should we close the hangar door?"

Tammy shook her head. "I like having the fresh air. Anyone have concerns about leaving the door open?" She stopped, looking around at each of the 19 people gathered in a circle of chairs. She waited a full minute before approaching the table and pipe. "When we meet, the pipe goes around the circle. It signifies that only truth will be spoken here." They waited as she smudged before packing and lighting the pipe, listening to the sound of rubber on concrete as Natalie's bike weaved and circled.

The sun was low when the van returned with their supper. By that time, they'd already decided on an exercise break, led by the MPs and Keely, who coaxed Natalie outside onto the concrete apron after clearing the excursion with Anna. The toddler's legs pushed her coaster bike along as they walked past several hangars, two fighter jets and a small helicopter. Keely stopped in the shade, stretching her back as Lauren approached and Natalie circled. Lauren asked, "You need a nap?"

Natalie said, "No."

Keely smiled. "Me, please." She watched Natalie while a Hercules transport landed in the distance. The child and the transport crisscrossed. "This could take all night."

Lauren said, "At least. I always kind of expected this would be the difficult part. Maybe it's because I enjoy doing more than talking. You ever met Tammy before?"

Keely shook her head.

Natalie said, "Tammy's my friend."

They looked at the child, who stopped in front of them, feet firmly on the ground. "Tammy likes coffee. My mom likes coffee. They drink coffee and talk. Sometimes they eat cookies. You like cookies?"

Lauren crouched down, back touching the hangar wall, eye

to eye with Natalie. "Chocolate chip are my favourite."

"I'm hungry." Natalie turned back the way they came.

Lauren followed, trailed by Keely who walked or waddled, depending on your particular sensibilities. When they reached the open mouth of the hangar door, a ragged line up formed at the rear of the van where the corporal arranged the table with aluminum containers of lasagna, salads, buns and dessert.

Lauren turned to a salivating Keely and said, "I don't think I've ever heard the word unprecedented used so many times by so many people. It may be time to get them thinking about phrases like at long last or it's about time."

Keely moved forward. "That lasagna smells like heaven. How about we eat first?"

Nigel and Hashir parked the white Ford on the west side of Branding Iron Mall. Named by a developer in Toronto–who had never been west of Brampton–it held more than 400 shops. Its attractions included a water park, a museum of all things tacky and a theme park where nursery rhymes were projected onto fibreglass rocks. The detectives walked under the BIM brand atop red metal tripod legs of steel and into entrance three. Hashir said, "My wife loves this place."

Nigel spoke into his phone. "Entering three. Are the other entrances covered?"

After each pair of officers confirmed their locations, Nigel said, "One through four converge on Teaze." He looked at Hashir. "You sure its Teaze?"

Hashir nodded, pointing at his tablet. "That's where the signal's coming from."

They walked past four children dancing over laser-projected gophers heading for holes painted on the tiled floor. The mall smelled of popcorn, cooking oil, cotton candy and tomahawk body spray when they passed a phalanx of ersatz cowboys heading east. They turned a corner, spotting the toy store on one side, and the glass walls of Teaze with Teas to Teaze your senses. Nigel recognized Brenda Bruciarsi with her phone at her ear. She watched their approach with disinterested acceptance. She wore a pink Queen's University hoodie. Nigel stopped, looking around, spotting his backup, anticipating a trap.

Brenda stood, picking up a yellow beach bag, moving toward the detectives. The men stopped, both checking the surroundings before focusing on her as she approached to within a metre.

Brenda lifted her chin, looked at them in turn. "You guys Calgary cops?"

Don't let her put you on the defensive. Nigel lifted the cuffs from his jacket pocket. "Detective Hashir will take your bag."

She shrugged while looking around, spotting six uniformed female officers approaching, surrendering her yellow bag to Hashir, holding her hands out front. "Is this really necessary? I mean you guys took long enough to find me."

Nigel snapped the cuffs on, then held up his hand and two female officers approached. Leong was dark-haired and Emerson was blonde. They proceeded to search Brenda for weapons before taking her by the elbows, moving toward the east exit.

Brenda said, "I'm not resisting." She looked over her shoulder at Hashir. "Take good care of my bag. You're going to want what's inside."

Nigel picked up the pace. Leong and Emerson did the same. Brenda said, "This has to be the most grotesque mall in the country. They say the only difference between yogurt and Calgary is that yogurt has a living culture. This place certainly is proof of that." She laughed at her joke.

It sounds forced. That's a good sign. Nigel held the glass door open, spotting the black and white SUV at the curb, moving toward it, waiting for Brenda to be buckled in by Emerson. Nigel climbed in on the passenger side while Leong climbed in behind the wheel. Nigel opened his window, looking at Hashir. "You and Emerson get the other vehicle and follow us."

Hashir nodded, turning, jogging back into the mall, Emerson following.

Nigel said, "Light it up, please."

Brenda said, "You should have leaned harder on Barrett. He was the only one I gave that number to. He's the most predictable. Self-preservation is his primary instinct."

They exited the parking lot, taking the long way around to give Hashir and Emerson time to catch up before heading for Stoney Trail. Nigel said, "You wanted us to find you."

Brenda looked out the window as they accelerated along the ramp. "Of course. Everyone would be watching airports and border crossings. Your people and their people. I know too much. My bosses used me to get their dirty jobs done. It would be naïve to assume I was the only one employed to do that kind of work. I will be seen as a threat to my bosses. This was my best option."

Nigel looked left at Leong. "Keep your eyes open. If they couldn't find her, they may have been watching us. Warn the others, please."

Leong lifted her chin, glancing in the mirror before reaching for her unit's mike. "Eyes up for 10-87."

Nigel heard Hashir's reply, "Confirm code 10-87?"

"Confirmed." Leong glanced at Nigel. "Should we request additional units?"

"Do it. Keep us away from other traffic as much as possible."

Leong increased her speed along a stretch of three lanes heading north.

Nigel looked over his shoulder, seeing Hashir closing to 50 metres behind them. "Eyes on any backup?"

Leong said, "Not yet."

A white Dodge Ram pickup pulled up on their right. The driver looked across, intent on the occupants in the marked SUV. His brown hair was styled and tipped with white highlights. The collar of his shirt was white. He kept both hands on the wheel as he accelerated in a cloud of diesel smoke.

Brenda said, "He's a scout. Former military. It's his job to confirm the target."

Nigel turned around, facing Brenda. "Get down." He reached for the unit's shotgun.

Leong took the handset, relaying a description of the pickup and its license.

Brenda leaned as far left as the seat belt would allow. "It'll happen fast. These guys are good. Five in the team. The guy in the pickup will already have contacted the others."

Leong looked in the rear view then her side mirror. "Two minivans approaching at speed."

Nigel nodded. "If you see a sliding door open, don't hesitate."

"Understood." She opened her window, putting her left hand on the wheel, lifting the Glock with her right, aiming it at the roof.

Nigel used his right hand to move the slide, chambering a round in the shotgun.

Leong said, "When they get close, I'll brake hard."

Nigel swung right in the seat, readying the shotgun, anticipating the most likely path of the minivan.

Emerson's voice came over the radio. "Two minivans just passed us. Rear doors open."

Leong rested her Glock on her left arm, punching the accelerator to the floor. "Let them think we're running."

Nigel looked ahead, spotting a clutch of vehicles about a kilometre ahead.

Leong glanced at the rear-view mirror. "They're separating. One on your side. The other on mine."

Nigel nodded, looking over his right shoulder.

One of the vans was silver. A red van was on Nigel's side. He saw the driver and the open side door behind. The barrel of a weapon was visible resting on the knee of the shooter in the rear seat.

Nigel braced the barrel against the door frame.

Leong hit the brakes.

Nigel got a glimpse of the driver's open mouth, the man in the rear seat wearing safety glasses, raising a weapon with an extended clip. Nigel fired once.

Leong fired.

Nigel saw the face of the man in the rear seat disappear in a bloody puff of buckshot and gore, weapon falling out the open door.

The driver of the red van braked momentarily before accelerating with the legs of his passenger dangling outside.

Leong said, "Way to go!"

The silver van was skidding sideways. Hashir's white sedan was accelerating, passing on the left after catching the van's rear bumper on the driver's side. The silver minivan began to roll, a blur of disintegrating machinery. It pirouetted, balancing momentarily on its nose, somersaulting into the ditch.

Hashir kept accelerating, pursuing the red van.

Leong holstered her Glock.

Nigel picked up the handset. "TA with injuries, two kilometres north of the Trans Canada. Vehicle in the ditch. Occupants armed and dangerous." He looked back in time to see Brenda puking onto the seat.

"She okay?" Leong asked.

"She's fine." Nigel chambered a second round in the shotgun, its barrel pointed out the open window.

Lauren sat next to Anna and Keely, holding their paper plates. They watched Natalie on her strider bike. Lauren stood. "How long will she go like that?"

Anna looked at her phone. "Around seven o'clock she'll fall asleep. Then she'll wake up at seven tomorrow morning."

Lauren walked over to the garbage can in the corner,

dumping their plates, returning.

Keely tapped her belly, "I'm hoping this one will sleep through the night."

Anna chuckled. "Be careful what you wish for, you might end up with a kid who goes nonstop for 12 hours all day every day."

Keely inhaled before standing. "Gotta pee."

Lauren asked, "How long do you think we'll be here?"

Keely shook her head. "As long as it takes for Tammy to get consensus."

Nigel, Hashir, Leong and Emerson were ordered to wait on scene for the Tactical escort. Nigel looked south at a line of traffic funneling into one lane. The shoulder and other two lanes were a tangled mass of marked and unmarked police units encircling the white pickup and red van. An ambulance was parked nearby with a fire engine. The HAWKS helicopter circled overhead.

Nigel watched the medical examiner's van with its rear hatch open. Two men loaded a bag with a headless corpse. *This is what Lane felt when he shot that psychopathic doctor.* He tried to analyze his feelings dispassionately, unable to get past the numbness.

"Open the door! Let me outta here! It stinks. It's getting hot in here!"

Nigel looked at Hashir who asked, "Is it wrong to feel like we made a mistake saving her life?"

Nigel shook his head, taking a couple of deep breaths before walking over to the ambulance. One of the EMTs sat on the bumper. "You got any wipes in there? You know something to clean up puke?"

The EMT stood, reaching inside, pulling out a packet of wipes. "Here you go."

"Thanks." Nigel took the wipes back to the SUV, tossing them through the open window to Brenda. "Here you go."

Brenda looked at the wipes on the seat.

Nigel backed away from the unit when he caught a whiff of the sour stink.

Brenda asked, "Don't you have people who do this kind of thing?"

He nodded. "You." Nigel stood next to Hashir and said, "Thank you man. You saved our asses back there."

Hashir shrugged. "It was a team effort. You took care of one van, we got the other." He looked at the red van and white truck. "Our guys did a nice job with the spike belts."

Emerson walked up to them. "Time to go." She looked past them at the Tactical's grey nondescript panel van.

Nigel nodded, walking toward the SUV.

Hashir took his shoulder. "Let me take her. You ride with Emerson. She's had enough of my driving." He took out his phone, typing a text.

Emerson pointed at a marked unit. "We'll take that one. I'm driving."

Nigel followed her. *It would be great to see Anna and Natalie right now.*

Emerson asked, "Have you phoned your family to let them know you're okay?"

"Not yet. I don't want to worry them. They went to Edmonton today."

Hashir said, "Here comes McEwan."

Staff Sergeant Corban McEwan was six foot four, short-haired, balding, 40, in better shape than most young cops and a man who refused to suffer fools. His green eyes locked on Nigel. "How are you?"

Nigel shrugged, trying to focus on the question, wondering how to describe the complex jumble of guilt, flashbacks, relief and tears. He wiped the back of his hand across his eyes.

McEwan moved to within three centimetres. "ASIRT is waiting at your office." He pointed at Hashir. "Detective

Wajdan?"

Hashir nodded. "Yes?"

"Can you take it from here? I'll be there to back you. It's your case."

Hashir lifted his eyebrows, looking at Nigel.

McEwan put his hand on Nigel's shoulder. "You're in shock. Go with the escort. Get the suspect tucked away. Talk to ASIRT. Then I want you to go home and get some rest. Understood?"

Nigel opened his mouth, unable to find words.

McEwan took Nigel by the elbow. "Come with me." He looked at Hashir. "I got this. You got Bruciarsi?"

"Yep." Hashir Wajdan turned, walking toward the SUV and their Tactical escort.

Lauren read the text on her phone. They sat in a circle with their after-supper brains on autopilot. She forced herself to focus on the message, handing the phone to Keely who read. When Keely was done, she handed the phone to Anna. She looked for her daughter who was doing lazy laps on her coaster bike. She got up, picking Natalie off the bike, parking it against a wall, holding the child close.

Tammy asked, "What is it?"

Lauren looked around the circle before focusing on Tammy. "This does not go beyond the circle?"

Tammy took a turn looking at each person. "Understood?" She waited for each person to respond.

Lauren said, "Four officers arrested Brenda Bruciarsi in Calgary. They were ambushed in transit. Two suspects were declared dead at the scene. Three survived. No officers were injured." She turned to look at Anna. "Anna's husband Nigel was there. We understand he is unharmed."

Tammy asked, "Who is this Brenda Bruciarsi?"

Keely said, "She–" she glanced at Lauren who nodded "–

worked for Prime Minister Ross. After the Ross scandal, she worked for WTF and CNIG who offered tax services to their clients. In effect, they helped wealthy North Americans hide money in offshore accounts like the Cayman Islands, Isle of Man and Cyprus; the very people we have been discussing this afternoon. We have evidence linking Bruciarsi and Kush Gumbay-Yaw–leader of the attack in Todos Santos–with Moby and Curtis Drayten. They are members of the exodus of wealthy individuals escaping to the Caymans. I believe the Drayten brothers ordered today's ambush because of what Bruciarsi knows of their illegal operations."

Lane said, "Women in this hangar have risked their lives to improve the lives of thousands of people in North America. None of the women here have benefited financially. Instead they have set up a bank to help others. How much more evidence do we need about the Untouchables?"

Tammy turned to Lauren. "This Bruciarsi, will she speak about her employers?"

Lauren said, "Hashir–my partner–will let me know."

Tammy stood. "Then we should wait until we have this information. I would like a walk to clear my mind." She moved to the open hangar door.

Lauren looked at her watch, seeing it was just after seven o'clock. She looked at Anna who was removing Natalie's helmet. The child's eyes were closed, cheek resting on her mother's shoulder.

YYC NEWS

<lead-in STEPHANIE OZDURAN> Police are investigating the scene of a shooting on Stoney Trail east. Natasha Summerville is there.

<cut to Natasha Summerville for standup> She has her red hair tied back and wears a green blouse. Behind her are several

police cars and the belly of an overturned minivan in the ditch.

"Northbound Stoney Trail has been blocked off for more than two hours as police investigate. Two people have died. One person was declared dead at the crash site behind me. The second in a vehicle two kilometres further along Stoney Trail.

"There are unconfirmed reports of shots being fired and weapons recovered at both scenes. It's also important to note Alberta Serious Incident Response Team–ASIRT as it is often referred to–is on site. Further details will be released as they become available.

"Back to you Stephanie.

<lead-out STEPHANIE OZDURAN> A spokesperson for Calgary Police has confirmed that four individuals are in custody and charges are pending. No further details were released.

It was dark when Nigel drove out of the parking lot alongside the police district offices. He headed north on Centre Street, intending to head west on Stoney Trail and home. Instead, he turned east, heading for Highway 2 North. By the time he reached Red Deer it was 11:00 pm. He stopped for gas then a cup of coffee. It was just off the highway in a strip mall. He went inside, stretching out the kinks from the road. He found himself second in line behind a bald guy wearing a goatee, a pink wife beater and shorts. A sand coloured iguana rested on his shoulder.

Nigel closed his eyes tight, opening them slowly. The iguana stuck its tongue out.

The barista said, "Espresso!"

A sixty-something woman in shorts, sandals and floral blouse picked up the drink, turning, spotting the iguana.

Nigel watched her eyes change from late night weary to wide awake query. She sipped her espresso, moving closer. "Hey mister? Can I pet your lizard?"

The man in orange turned, seeing the grandmother. "If you like."

The laughter didn't jump out of Nigel, it pole-vaulted.

The iguana did a 180, diving down the neck of orange man's shirt who said, "Drake!"

Grandmother said, "That's not what I meant!"

Nigel shook his head, putting his hand up in an effort to apologize, unable to speak.

After he got his coffee, he went to the car, setting the cup in a holder, closing his eyes, leaning the seat back. *Maybe I should close my eyes for a couple of minutes.*

Lauren stepped back in the hangar with a clearer mind after the walk with Tammy, who'd asked, "Will you be offended if this is a quiet walk?"

They had walked for an hour in and around the buildings on the base, stopping to watch aircraft land and take off before returning to the hangar where cots had been set up. Tammy dragged her cot outside and lay down, eyes on the stars.

Lauren sat down next to Anna who cuddled with Natalie. She watched Keely sit up, putting her feet on the ground, heading for the washroom.

Lauren's phone vibrated. She read a text message from Rhonda.

Nigel shot and killed a suspect today. After the ASIRT interview, McEwan sent Nigel home. A unit checked on him later. Nigel not at home. Phone is off. Please advise if he contacts you or Anna.

CHAPTER 14

Willcock got out of the shower and read a text from Ishmael.

Proceed to Edmonton. Eliminate Catrinas. Previous attempts unsuccessful. Incentives will be deposited in your account upon successful completion. Target location to follow.

It took a few minutes to work out the incentive total. Full payment on the property in Costa Rica took a little over an hour.

Nigel opened the front door to his parent's house, walking inside, seeing his mother's open-eyed corpse. He turned when he heard knuckles on glass. The door was open. He saw his father and screamed.

He opened his eyes. The face on the other side of the glass was so close it made Nigel recoil.

The uniformed RCMP officer stepped back, hands on belt. "Sir, please step out of the vehicle."

Nigel blinked, opening his door.

"How much have you had to drink sir?" the officer asked.

Nigel stood, wincing at the pain in his lower back. "I haven't been drinking." He focused on the officer's dark hair, moustache and cleft chin. "I fell asleep."

The officer pointed at the Second Cup. "The owner of the coffee shop heard screaming coming from this vehicle. She called us."

"I'm on my way to Edmonton. It was late." Nigel smiled. "Long day."

"Can I see your ID?"

Nigel reached into his shirt pocket, handing it to the officer who studied Nigel's licence and CPS ID.

"You're with the Calgary police?"

"Yes."

The RCMP officer handed back the ID. "We've received an alert to keep a look out for you. Is your phone on?"

Nigel shook his head. "I shut it off."

"ASIRT up your ass?"

Nigel tried to smile, instead he felt tears on his cheeks. "I had to shoot a guy."

"Okay if I buy you a coffee? I'm due for a break. Do me a favour and turn your phone on."

Nigel nodded, unable to respond.

Hashir stared at his computer screen, mind somewhere else. He knew if someone asked him what he was thinking he would be lost for an answer. A hand touched his shoulder. He turned.

McEwan said, "I read the report. It looks good." He pointed to the front of the office. "I sent Rhonda home. She mentioned Zena has a soccer game later today. Go home, get some sleep, be at your daughter's soccer game."

Hashir stood. "Any news on Nigel?"

"On his way to Edmonton to see Anna and Natalie. The RCMP found him asleep in a parking lot out front of a coffee shop. The member bought him a coffee and sent Nigel on his way."

Hashir leaned his head back. "How about you?"

"I'm fine. I'll call if I need anything. You go. See Zena's game."

Lane sat just outside the hangar door, sipping coffee from a paper cup. Christine brought a chair, plopping it next to him.

Lane asked, "Hear from the kids?"

She smiled. "Alexandra texted me this morning, saying they had a good weekend. Matt let her sleep in Sunday morning. Said it was heaven to get up at 9:00 am." She leaned her head against his shoulder. "How did you sleep?"

"The colonel snores and the hangar's like an echo chamber."

"I can't wait to go home and sleep in my own bed. I miss Dan and the kids."

Lane looked out at the runway as a transport taxied before taking off. "Tammy came to talk with me earlier."

"What about?"

He took a sip. "I'm dying for a mochaccino. Anyway, she asked why you and I had been quiet during the discussions. I explained we were listening, trying to get the big picture. I told her I thought we might actually be at the beginning of some strange new revolution." He took another sip. "Then she said she hoped this revolution wouldn't shed as much blood as previous ones."

Christine took Lane's cup and a sip. "I think she might be right. Two people were killed in Mexico. Two more yesterday in Calgary. Do you think Tammy will be able to pull it off by bringing us all together?"

Lane shrugged, standing. "She has a reputation for doing just that. You want another coffee?"

Christine nodded, standing. "I'll come with you."

He closed his eyes, soaking up the morning sun. "Okay."

Willcock sent a text to her supplier. She turned off the phone before boarding a direct flight to Edmonton.

Lauren sat on her cot with her back against the hangar wall, sipping coffee, nibbling on a peanut butter and marmalade bagel. Natalie was on her bike. By now they were all watching out for her, stepping aside or stopping mid-stride almost without thinking. Lauren smiled at the way Natalie had managed to train them.

Her phone vibrated. She set her coffee on the concrete, picking up the phone, reading a text from McEwan.

Nigel on his way to you. Bruciarsi claims to have detailed evidence on her various employers.

We are in the process of verifying evidence and working with the Crown prosecutor on charges. Prepare for any eventuality.

Lauren got up, showing the text to Anna and Keely sitting next to one another eating their breakfasts.

Anna asked, "What's Nigel's problem? I haven't heard a word from him." She pulled out her phone, tapping a text.

Tammy stood next to Corporal Crowshoe who was on his radio. She said, "Let's get together after breakfast. Anyone here know a Nigel Li?"

Natalie said, "Daddy!"

Even Anna smiled at the eruption of laughter echoing out the hangar door.

Nigel walked inside. Natalie ran for her father, hugging him around the knees.

Tammy watched from where she sat.

Lauren thought, *Nigel? You look like shit.*

Anna wrapped them in a group hug. Nigel put his head on her shoulder. Some looked away as he sobbed. Tammy set her plate down, walking over to the back of the food van, getting a plate, filling it, waiting about a metre away from Anna and her family. They separated, Nigel wiping at his eyes, looking around with embarrassment, Natalie tucking her head against his neck.

Tammy said, "He needs food. Sit down. Eat. Would you like some coffee?"

Nigel looked at Tammy, then at Anna who pointed, "This is Tammy and this is Nigel."

He nodded, reaching for a sausage, inhaling it.

The sound of jet engines made them turn. A green Challenger jet with Canadian flags on the nose taxied, easing alongside the white jet. The jet's engines shut down.

Nigel took another sausage.

The door of the jet opened.

Nigel took a baking powder biscuit, opening it with his free hand, setting a sausage on one half, folding it, stuffing the mini sandwich in his mouth.

A grey-haired officer in a green uniform and black beret stepped onto the concrete as the jet's engines slowed. He marched into the shade. Lauren saw the yellow flashes on his sleeves, red flashes on his collars, yellow Canadian flags and one crown on his shoulders.

"Who's in charge here?"

Everyone turned to Tammy.

Colonel Russell saluted, "I am, General Fildebrandt."

Fildebrandt asked, "Where are the prisoners?"

Tammy said, "There are none."

Fildebrandt spoke at her without making eye contact. "Who the hell are you and what's this? Some kind of séance?"

Lauren said, "It's a meeting. A pipe ceremony. We're working on a problem."

Anna looked up from her phone. "You are General Ralph Fildebrandt?"

He turned to look down at her. "And who are you?"

"Back off," Lauren said.

Nigel chewed, making a step toward the General. Lauren used her free hand to grab Nigel by the elbow. She turned to Lane for help. He walked over, putting an arm around Nigel's shoulders, saying something only Nigel could hear.

Fildebrandt pointed at Anna while looking at Russell. "Why is she not under arrest?"

Anna looked at her phone. "You are an investor with WTF and CNIG?"

Fildebrandt turned on her. "That is confidential information!"

Tammy asked, "You do recognize Manpreet Singh, the Minister of Defence?"

Manpreet stepped out of the hallway, into the main hangar, wiping her hands on her black slacks.

"Hello General Fildebrandt. Is there a problem?"

"Actually, yes." Keely stood, walking to stand next to Tammy. "General Fildebrandt, are you aware that Brenda Bruciarsi was arrested yesterday?" She held up her phone. "We are receiving updates about her ongoing interrogation and disclosures." She turned to Lauren who nodded.

Fildebrandt asked, "What does she have to do with this situation? I gave an order and it will be carried out."

Nigel asked, "What was your order?"

Lauren said, "He wanted Russell to arrest us and send Natalie with social services."

Nigel spat bits of biscuit. "What kind of skullfuckery is this?! My daughter and Anna?" He pointed at Lane, Laura and Christine. "These people risked their lives. Bruciarsi and the Drayten's tried to kill them. And yesterday, I had to kill one of their hired killers! You sit in your Ottawa office and give orders like this! What kind of douchebag, dumb-fuck, asshole…"

He glanced at Tammy who raised her eyebrows and he

stopped.

Natalie said, "Daddy, you said fuck."

Lauren looked around. She saw the MPs lining up behind Colonel Russell as others were forming up on the opposite side.

Tammy strolled into the middle of it all. She moved in close to the General. Her quiet voice silenced the room.

"General Fildebrandt, on your honour as a warrior, do you have money in…" She glanced at Anna.

Anna said, "An Isle of Man account."

Fildebrandt looked at Anna's phone, then the eyes of the soldiers. He looked back at Tammy. "Yes, and they assured me no laws were broken."

Manpreet Singh said, "I will accept your resignation."

Lauren said, "Just a minute here. You said no laws were broken?"

Fildebrandt asked, "Who are you?"

"A detective who was shot at by hired killers."

Tammy asked, "Did you order the 45s to attack any of the people in this room?"

Fildebrandt shook his head. "No."

Keely asked, "Do you know who Willcock is?"

Fildebrandt asked, "What do you know about Willcock?"

Keely said, "A freelancer working for Bruciarsi."

Fildebrandt looked away. "I know of Willcock."

Keely asked, "Did Willcock tell you where to find us?"

"Yes. Sent me a text."

Keely said, "Willcock works for the Drayten boys. Intel indicates they ordered the attacks in Todos Santos and Calgary."

Tammy said, "You can join us if you like. No one in this room is going to be arrested today." She stood there, waiting for him to reply.

Fildebrandt looked at Manpreet Singh who had her arms crossed, standing next to Mary Starblanket, Minister of Justice and Attorney General of Canada. Fildebrandt pointed at Lauren and Anna. "They stole my money."

Lane asked, "How did they profit?"

"What?"

"They collected overdue taxes. The money went to a virtual bank. One of their initiatives is to provide clean drinking water in North America. None of the people here have profited from the transfer of funds into the VBank. They can prove it. The money is being used to improve the lives of others."

Lauren looked at Fildebrandt's ring finger. "Are you in the process of getting a divorce?"

The general's eyes zeroed in on her. "That's private."

Anna said, "You have $8.3 million remaining in your Isle of Man account."

Lauren asked, "Hiding it from the divorce settlement?"

Fildebrandt glanced at the men in uniform. "Carry on then." He turned, marching outside.

Ella said, "Stop it!"

Alexandra ran upstairs to find her niece's wet hair dripping on the bathroom floor.

Alexandra grabbed a towel. "What happened?"

Ella pushed hair from eyes as her aunt rubbed her hair dry. "Indy poured water on me."

"Indy? Come here? Why did you pour water on your sister?" Alexandra dropped the towel on the floor, using her foot to move the towel over the wet linoleum.

"She broke my Lego!"

He stood in the door with a broken Millenium Falcon. "It has 1329 pieces and she broke it. Tio Matt helped me build it. Now it's ruined."

Only Indy would remember exactly how many pieces are in the whateverthefuckyoucallit. "We'll put all the pieces in a box and ask Tio to help you put it back together."

Ella said, "It was an accident!"

Indy asked, "Can you ask Tio to come home now?"

The baby started to cry.

Ella asked, "When is Mommy coming home? I miss her."

Alexandra stood there for a moment, concentrating on breathing. She picked up Ella. "Your Mom is coming home soon. I need to get Karen. Can you help me?"

Ella nodded, putting her head on her aunt's shoulder. "I miss my Mom."

"She said she'd call tonight." *I need a break.*

Brenda Bruciarsi's orange coveralls had rolled up sleeves. She shuffled along the linoleum in white flip-flops, hands in cuffs. She plopped into a metal chair, crossing one leg over the other.

McEwan sat with one elbow on the table.

Brenda said, "I would like a cup of tea and one other thing."

"What's that?"

"Detective Hashir doing the interview." She looked at the camera.

"How come?"

"He saved my life. Either him or Nigel." She waved at the camera.

"I'm afraid both of them are unavailable."

She pushed hair over her right ear. "Then you'd better make one of them available. Those two have balls and oddly enough, I trust them. I understand the agreement my lawyer made with the Crown Prosecutor. If you want the password to my laptop with the taped conversations, emails, texts and documents, then one of those detectives needs to be here. I see by your expression you think I'm being ridiculous. I don't care what you think. You get one of them in here if you want the password."

Brenda mimed zipping her mouth shut.

Willcock handed the taxi driver a $100 bill, walking over to the black two-door, short box four-by-four pickup. It was parked next to a pillar on the south side of the mall. The key fob was atop rear tire.

On the passenger seat, Willcock opened the black case. The micro Uzi was nestled in a foam cut out. The paper bag under the seat held six clips of 32 rounds each. Behind the seat there was a yellow box with a black pair of SWAT boots. The size nines were a precise fit.

Hashir and Zena sat in the car eating ice cream. His was chocolate silk, hers bubblegum. She wore her green and black soccer uniform. Her black hair was tied back in a ponytail.

She said, "You mad at me because I got a penalty?"

He shook his head, enjoying the luxury of sharing ice cream. "What did she say to you?"

She lifted her eyebrows. "She asked me if I had a bomb."

"What? You were born here. That's why you elbowed her?"

"Yes. Coach said she was just trying to get me off my game. That I shouldn't let her get under my skin like that."

He shook his head, looking out the windshield at people going into and out of Maddie's Ice Cream.

"What?"

"I wish I'd known."

Zena asked, "What would you have done?"

Hashir's phone rang. He reached into his pocket, pulling out the phone, reading the name. "I have to take this."

She nodded, licking the ice cream, tongue turning blue.

"What's up?"

McEwan said, "Bruciarsi will only speak with you or Nigel.

He's in Edmonton. Did you get the game in?"

"Yes."

"Well?"

Hashir looked sideways at Zena pretending to concentrate on her ice cream.

She said, "I'm coming with you. Let's go."

McEwan said, "Of course. Bring Zena," then he hung up.

Tammy looked around the circle. Shadows stretched their legs across the taxiway. "From the beginning these negotiations have been aimed at creating consensus. That takes time and it means everyone will be heard. I think we should break for supper. We might be able to finish up after that if you are willing."

Natalie said, "Let's eat!"

Hashir sat across from Brenda Bruciarsi in the grey room with its metal chairs, bland walls and cameras behind him. He resisted the impulse to look over his shoulder with a nod to Brenda's lawyer, the Crown Prosecutor, McEwan and an RCMP officer who'd flown in from Ottawa. They all watched the video from separate locations. He wondered if Zena would be entertained by the video games their tech guy had set up for her.

He watched Brenda sip her tea. *Let's get started.* "The password?"

"You get right to the point. Good. It's millafiori." She spelled the password out.

Hashir knew the password was being checked as he spoke. If it didn't work there would be a knock on the door. "Is there anything else we need to know?"

"I don't think so. It's all there. I've organized it with separate folders for separate employers. Their conversations, emails, texts and relevant video. They are all listed by name. My bank statements have a separate folder as well."

"Why did you ask for me?"

"You could have let those guys kill me. You didn't. I owe you."

Hashir reached for a bottle of water, twisting off the cap, sipping, putting the cap back on.

She said, "The password is correct."

Hashir shrugged. "We'll see."

Lauren stood up, walking over to Tammy who sat eating beef on a bun for supper.

Lauren crouched, knees popping. "You know there's a fire pit out behind one of the old wooden hangars. I could find where the wood is kept. Maybe we could get together around a fire and change things up a bit."

Tammy nodded, wiping her mouth with a paper napkin. "I like it."

In the dusk's half-light Ursula Concordia wore a ball cap, black hoodie, black yoga pants, eye shadow and lip-gloss, holding a selfie stick and smart phone.

"This is Ursula Concordia of Mustang Media, inside the security fence at Canada Forces Base Edmonton. We have reliable reports of a secret meeting of lefties, thieves and snowflakes happening inside. Federal cabinet members are here with several Canadians accused of stealing trillions of dollars from offshore accounts. The biggest theft in history and Mustang Media is here via Periscope investigating another one of this government's all-inclusive snowflake meetings they're so proud of."

She turned the camera 180 degrees. "You can see a gathering of what I estimate to be twenty individuals sitting in lawn chairs around a fire. I have been told they include five ringleaders from the infamous ultra-violent, alt-left group known as the Catrinas. I am here to expose this secret meeting and shed some light on the people behind the biggest robbery in history."

She moved on soft soles. "I will attempt to get in close enough to hear what they are saying. Perhaps we will get some answers to the AQ while I'm here."

"What is this AQ?"

Ursula stopped, looking to her left. "Who are you? You scared me. You are making me uncomfortable. You are inside my bubble." She made a semicircle with her free right hand.

Lauren said, "We heard you cutting a hole in the fence." A hummingbird whirred past her ear.

Ursula looked right. "Who are you? I'm with Mustang Media. I have a right to be here."

"My name is Tammy Crowchild."

"And I am Lauren Jackson. I believe Tammy asked you a question." Lauren stood between Ursula, the fire and the phone on the end of its selfie stick.

Ursula looked over Lauren's shoulder. "I am Ursula Concordia with Mustang Media. I am here investigating reports of a secret meeting."

Tammy nodded. "Yes. You said that. Please answer the question."

Ursula asked, "What question?"

Tammy asked, "What does AQ mean?"

Ursula said, "Aboriginal Question."

Tammy said, "I am Aboriginal from Tsuu T'ina Nation. Ask your question."

Ursula said, "It's not a question really. It's a statement about Aboriginals."

Tammy asked, "Do you always reduce human beings to acronyms?"

Ursula tried to turn her camera on Tammy. "I am on Periscope. This is live! People know I'm here."

Tammy said, "Yes, Periscope is a live broadcast. We know this. We also know you illegally entered a military base. Are you a terrorist?"

Ursula glared at Tammy. "I'm no terrorist!"

"Why not come in through the front gate?"

A tawny orange-throated hummingbird hovered a metre from Lauren's nose.

Tammy moved toward the fire. "Come here. I would like to show you something."

Ursula looked at the fire's light. "Taxpayers have a right to know!"

Tammy stood close to the circle of people in chairs around the campfire, their faces yellowed by the fire.

Ursula pointed her camera at Tammy who said, "There will be a statement for the media as soon as the reporters arrive. I estimate it will take half an hour." Tammy nodded at Lauren. "UC? I think the MPs want to speak with you."

"UC?" Ursula asked.

Lauren pointed at Ursula.

They turned at the sound of an approaching Yukon, headlights illuminating the gathering, MPs climbing out. One said, "We've detected a breach."

Ursula moved the phone around, aiming at the MPs. She pointed at the blond and blue-eyed officer. "I want that one."

Lauren noted how Ursula's tone of voice changed with the arrival of the MPs. She noticed Ursula's combat boots set shoulder width apart, knees bent. *Why is she adopting a firing stance?*

Ursula's right hand reached into her bag.

Lauren reacted. Her palm struck Ursula's sternum. Her

right foot hooked behind Ursula's knee. As they fell, the bag dropped away, an Uzi appeared.

Lauren grabbed Ursula's right forearm with her left, then with both hands as the weapon spat. Lauren instinctively wedged her right elbow under Ursula's chin, fighting the recoil, concentrating on keeping the arm and the weapon aimed skyward.

She felt another body knock into hers. A knee slammed into her cheek. Lauren held on.

Lane handed Lauren a towel. She wrapped it around the plastic bag of ice, pressing it against her swollen cheek. The base doctor had already checked her over, giving her the obligatory list of concussion symptoms.

Lane asked, "How's the cheek?"

"Tender." She closed her eyes, inhaling, remembering her yoga breathing.

"How did you know?"

She opened her eyes. "Know what?"

Lane looked around at the various media types. Their lights filled the interior of the hangar with long shadows as reporters took their positions.

"Something wasn't right. Her makeup and those boots. The way she looked around. She acted nervous but her eyes reminded me of someone else."

"The grand dragon?"

She nodded. "Calculating is the word that comes closest to it, I guess."

Lane recalled the eyes of the man he killed. "Calculating works." *For want of a better word.*

Tammy appeared from a corner of the hangar, standing in front of the microphones wearing her jeans and a handmade knit sweater. Four federal ministers took up positions on her right and left. The reporters focused on Tammy because of her reputation for being brief.

She looked into the cameras and said, "Thank you for coming on such short notice. A group of Canadians have been meeting over the last two days, discussing what to do about the money recovered by a group called the Catrinas. Our estimates put the total at $17.3 trillion. An independent accounting firm has confirmed the amount and it has determined the total taken coincides with taxes and interest owed to Canadian, Mexican and US governments. The money has been deposited in a not-for-profit virtual bank with a mandate to improve the economic well-being of North American citizens. Its first act is to commit $2.3 trillion toward providing clean and safe drinking water to all North Americans. The remaining $15 trillion will be invested in capital projects and individual bursaries aimed at generating sustainable profits and improved economic status for low income families. The governments of Canada, Mexico and the US have agreed not to prosecute the Catrinas because they have not profited from the recovery of the funds. Again, independent accountants have assured us the Catrinas have deposited all confiscated funds into the V-Bank. I will now ask Minister of Finance, Robert MacWhirter to answer any specific questions you may have about this massive transfer of funds into V-Bank."

Tammy stepped back from the microphone.

A female reporter with blonde hair asked, "Minister Crowchild? Can you confirm the armed attack on police officers in Calgary on Monday of this week was linked to this case?"

Tammy nodded, leaning into the microphone. "I can confirm it." She sat down, indicating with her hand that Robert should carry on.

A male reporter asked, "Will you comment on reports of gunfire at this base?"

Tammy shrugged, mouth closed, waiting, eyes focused on MacWhirter who said, "An armed assailant was neutralized. There were no casualties. The matter is in the early stages of investigation."

CHAPTER 15

Lauren was behind the wheel of Nigel's car. Anna sat in the passenger seat. Nigel sat next to Natalie in the back seat.

Anna asked, "You sure you're okay to drive?"

Lauren nodded. "It beats the hell outta flyin'." She checked the rear-view mirror. "She asleep?"

Nigel brushed Natalie's cheek with the back of his hand. "More like comatose. She could sleep through a tornado."

Lauren asked, "How you feeling now?"

Anna turned with her back to the door so she could see Nigel.

Nigel filled his cheeks with air, holding his hands up in a gesture of surrender.

Anna said, "That's no answer."

Nigel said, "I killed a guy. Blew his fucking head off."

Lauren asked, "How many in your vehicle?"

"Three."

Lauren looked ahead, flashing her high beams at a car approaching on the four-lane divided highway. The approaching car's headlights dimmed. "And in Hashir's?"

Nigel looked out his window. "Two."

Lauren said, "I had to kill a guy a couple of days ago. Christine hit him in the head with a drone. He was reaching for his gun. There was a split second. I put two in his chest and one in his throat. You know, it hasn't hit me yet. Maybe it won't. I don't know. Lane talked with me after. He said he finally came around to understanding that we do what we have to do. That is all. He said it's one of those simply complex, horrible situations. You do your job and do what you have to do."

Anna watched Nigel. "You're having flashbacks about your mom?"

He nodded.

"Nigel was a kid when he came home to find his mother's body. His father murdered her."

Lauren said, "Shit! Sorry Nigel. I didn't know."

Nigel said, "How could you? I don't talk about it. I guess this has triggered the old trauma. I just had to see Anna and Natalie. It was like this single-minded, all I could think about, crazy fucking obsession."

Lauren checked the lights of the rental SUV in her rear view. "You want me to ride with Lane and Christine?"

Nigel tapped her on the shoulder. "That's not what I'm saying at all. You drive. We can talk. Maybe it'll help. Maybe it'll stop the flashbacks. A whole lot of maybes right now."

Anna put her hand on Lauren's shoulder, "Thanks for what you did back there. That crazy bitch would have killed us all."

Nigel said, "We owe you."

Christine drove the rented Ford SUV. Her uncle sat next to her.

Lane asked, "You want me to drive?"

"I'm good. I just want to be there before the kids wake up. I hope Alex and the baby are okay."

"Thank you for coming after me."

Christine glanced at him before returning to focus on the road ahead. A string of red taillights stretched three kilometres in front of her. She knew the closest set belonged to Anna and

Nigel's car. "You're not mad?"

"Not anymore."

"We were losing you. You were fading. I don't even know the right words for it. You were losing weight, going through the motions of living. I knew someone had to bring you back."

"From where?"

She smiled. "We're not talking Mexico."

"What are we talking then?"

Her right hand touched his left forearm. "We need you. Arthur's gone and we need you."

He lifted his chin. The yellow lights of a row of gas stations on the south side of Red Deer became visible. "Okay. Feel like a coffee?"

Lauren saw the headlights flashing in her rear view. "Looks like they want us to stop."

Anna's phone rang and she answered it, listening. "Okay." She pointed to the right. "They want us to pull over for a coffee."

Nigel laughed. "Lane and his fucking coffee!"

Lauren opened the door to her two-storey condo backing onto a park and bike path running down to the Bow River. She turned, watching Anna drive away. It was 3:30 am.

Lauren locked the door behind her, parking her luggage next to the closet, kicking off her shoes, hearing snoring.

She stopped. The snoring came from the downstairs living room. She tiptoed into the dining room, peering over the railing. The moonlight shone its pale light on the person sleeping under her grandmother's handmade quilt. The person snored. The rattling snort sounded familiar. "Ian?"

Christine took off her shoes, moving into the kitchen.

Lane followed, waiting as she turned on the light.

Matt's voice came from the living room. "Christine? We're in here."

Christine and Lane tiptoed through the kitchen and into the hallway. Matt sat in the easy chair. Karen was nestled with her head resting on his shoulder. "Everyone's asleep."

Lane smiled, touching Matt's cheek then Karen's. "She's beautiful."

Matt smiled, eyes filling with tears, nodding at Lane.

Christine turned, heading for the stairs. "I'm gonna check on Indy and Ella."

Lane reached out. "Okay if I hold her and you get some sleep?"

Matt leaned forward, standing, handing over his daughter. "That would be great. She's been waking up at three every morning. Alexandra is beat."

Lane tucked Karen up against his shoulder, changing places with Matt.

"Good to have you home safe."

"Your sister is a tiger."

Matt smiled. "Don't I know it."

Lauren woke to the smell of coffee. She opened her eyes, staring at the stippled ceiling, seeing the eyes of the man she killed as he choked, coughing up blood. She lifted the covers, sitting up, heading for the washroom before going downstairs.

Ian sat at the kitchen table, sipping coffee, reading the news on his laptop. His brown hair was coloured neon green, his eyes were grey instead of her green, his face more angelic and triangular. "Hey Lauren." He stood as she came downstairs, almost a head shorter as he hugged her. He was ten pounds lighter than her and worked hard at keeping fit.

"I made some coffee. There's yogurt and fresh fruit in the fridge." He looked at his wristwatch. "You've got an hour."

"Thanks," she said, heading for the coffee machine and pouring herself a cup. *An hour?* "How did you know when I'd be home?"

He leaned a hip against the dishwasher. "I'll never tell."

Lauren sipped the black. "Rhonda?"

He shrugged, looking over his shoulder at the laptop.

"Hashir?"

"Better have some breakfast." He sniffed. "And a shower. Your travelling clothes are already in the wash."

She set her cup on the counter, opening the fridge door, reaching for raspberries and yogurt. "Thanks for the groceries." She set the containers on the counter, opening a cupboard door, grabbing a bowl. "I told you I'm not going."

"Kate knew you'd say that." He handed her his phone. "She wants to talk to you."

Lauren shook her head. "I killed a man. I can't go." She took out a spoon, digging into the container, transferring the Greek yogurt into her bowl. "You know what I'm like. I handle what I have to when I have to. Everyone thinks I'm taking it well. Then I get into some other stressful situation and melt down." She added raspberries to the yogurt before sitting down across from Ian. "Going back to Kenton after all these years definitely qualifies as a stressful situation. Katie will get over it."

"Good luck with that." Ian looked at the ceiling.

"What do you mean?"

"Mom thought you might need convincing. She flew in yesterday. She's sleeping in your guest room. Didn't you wonder why I was on the couch?" He lifted his eyebrows. "And you're the detective in the family?"

Lane carried two backpacks – one red, the other pink – down the hill leading to the Bow River valley. The leaves were just out on the trees, their canopy hiding much of the city under an emerald cloak. Indy and Ella waited at the corner with the scooters their father bought them while Lane and Christine were away.

Ella asked, "What did you get us?" for the third time.

Lane shifted the backpacks, feeling a sweaty patch on the back of his shirt. "There wasn't any time for shopping but I've been thinking…"

Indy asked, "What?"

"You know that toy store in Kensington?"

Ella nodded. "Near the coffee shop you like?"

He smiled. "Maybe we could go there after school and get something then?"

Ella said, "Better ask my mom first." She pressed the button on the light pole. Yellow lights flashed over the crosswalk.

"Look both ways." He stepped between them, looking west and east before crossing. They scooted ahead to the sidewalk then south to Queen Mary School.

Lane watched them race. His chest began to swell with joy. He savoured the sensation, hurrying to catch up to the kids.

"Mom! The speed limit is 110 kilometres per hour."

Ian sat in the passenger seat as they passed a semi with a bison painted on its side. The parallel lines of divided, four lane highway met at the eastern horizon. White clouds were beginning to form against the prairie blue. Fields of recently sown crops sprouted their initial green.

"There's a lot of work to do before the rehearsal dinner."

Lauren leaned left, checking the speedometer. "Swift

Current has an RCMP detachment."

Sylvia Jackson was born and raised in Saskatchewan, wavering around 180 pounds. At five and a half feet she had dyed brown short cut hair and green eyes. She puffed from a blue vaping cigarette, filling the cabin with a chemical apple scent. "I've never had a speeding ticket," she waved away the vape cloud with her right hand. "Both of you have, so shut it!"

The siren and flashing lights came up behind them a little over five minutes later.

Sylvia said, "Shit!" as she lifted her foot off the accelerator before easing over the rumble strips, creating a dust cloud as she drove on the shoulder and stopped. "Hand me my purse!"

Lauren picked up her mother's mauve purse, heaving it in between the front seats of her Tacoma, keeping her hands in view as the officer walked up to the passenger door.

Ian powered his window down.

Lauren heard the officer's boots on the gravel, then saw her face as she spotted Ian's neon green hair. The woman leaned on the door, looking at Sylvia and Lauren.

Sylvia asked, "Is there a problem officer?"

The officer lifted her eyebrows. She looked to be forty and had her black hair tied back. "You were traveling 60 kilometres per hour over the posted speed limit in a work zone. I need to see your license, registration and insurance please."

Sylvia reached into her purse, pulling out her wallet, opening three zippers while vaping, filling the cabin with that chemical apple smell.

Lauren gagged. "Ian, the rest is in the glove compartment."

Sylvia handed her license over. The officer read the name and asked, "Are you the registered owner of the vehicle?"

Sylvia puffed. "No. It's my daughter's truck. She's a detective in Calgary you know. She's had a hard time. Had to kill a guy in Mexico. Don't worry, it was in self-defence. We're on our way to a wedding in Kenton. My youngest is getting married. We need to be there for the rehearsal."

Lauren's mouth filled with saliva. She reached for the door

handle, getting out and to her feet, bending at the waist, vomiting over the grass. She felt her brother's hand on her back as he said, "Remind you of any other family road trips?"

Lauren had a well-earned reputation for all kinds of motion sickness. Sitting in the back seat was bad. Driving with a smoker plus the negative g-force of the downside of a hill was worse. Fried foods were a no no. Any one or a combination of those often induced sudden, violent reactions.

Ian handed her a bottle of water then a wipe from a pack her mother carried in her purse. It took her ten minutes of strolling through the long grass in the ditch, sipping, spitting out the water and cleaning her face with wipes before she felt like walking back to her truck. "I'm driving."

Sylvia sat next to her purse on the Tacoma's tailgate. She puffed a vape cloud and waved the ticket in Lauren's face. "She gave me a ticket for $798."

Lauren gagged, covering her mouth as she passed through the chemical apple cloud. "And put that fucking thing away!"

Sylvia opened her mouth, thought better of it, dropping the vape cigarette in her purse, pushing herself off the tailgate. She marched around the passenger side, climbing in the back seat.

Lauren slammed the tailgate closed, checking for traffic, walking up the driver's side, wedging herself in, moving the seat back. They drove the rest of the way to Regina in silence.

Lane waited outside the east facing doors of Queen Mary Elementary School. The kids' scooters leaned against the chain link fence to his left. He looked right at the stand of 40-metre-tall poplar trees. He heard the school's outside buzzer ring then turned, waiting for the door to open. Indy was first out, walking toward his uncle, handing over the backpack.

"Okay if we play then go to the toy store?"

Lane looked at his watch. "How long?"

Indy looked over his shoulder, checking to see which friends were nearby. "Fifteen minutes?"

"Okay." Lane set the timer on his phone.

Ella arrived a minute later, setting her backpack on Lane's toes, grabbing her scooter. She lifted her chin, frowning. "You promised we could go to the toy store."

"Indy asked to play with his friends."

"I can't wait that long!" Her arms were wings, swooping, slapping her thighs. She turned to her brother, yelling, "You are a dickhead!" Turning to Lane, "You promised!"

"Hey Ella." A woman with dark, curly, shoulder-length hair approached. She wore jeans and a blue blouse. She held out her hand to Lane.

"I'm Michelle. Natalie and Mateis's mom." She nodded in the direction of Indy and a girl with red hair. They were running the wrong way up the slide. Michelle crouched eye to eye with Ella. "Mateis would like to play." She pulled a granola bar from her purple purse. "Hungry?"

Ella nodded. Michelle unwrapped the bar, handing it to Ella who bit off the end before walking toward the playground.

Michelle stood, turning to Lane. "Mateis said one of the girls told Ella she didn't want to be her friend anymore."

"Ouch. Thanks for the heads-up." Lane watched as Ella finished off the granola, then headed for the monkey bars. She reached up, grabbing each bar, swinging her legs, working her way across. *On Saturday I was in the middle of a gun battle. Four days later and it's playground drama.*

"What's funny?" Michelle asked.

"Was I smiling?"

"You were."

Lane lifted his chin in Ella's direction. "I was in Mexico on the weekend. Now I'm here. The change in realities is jarring."

"In a good way?"

He nodded. "Definitely."

Ella hung upside down, legs hooked over a bar. Indy and Natalie ran across a bridge joining one slide to another.

Michelle said, "Almost everyone I know is following the story about the Catrinas. How they took trillions of dollars from offshore tax havens. Any of that happen near you?"

"I didn't see much of it." *My face was in the dirt and I was covered with debris from a shredded bougainvillea.*

Michelle waited, watching him.

He studied her expression. "You talked with Christine."

Michelle smiled. "Natalie recognized her under all that Catrina makeup."

"Did she tell you about the drone?"

Michelle frowned. "No."

"The Catrinas took care of three of the four 45s. You know what a 45 is?"

"Not really."

"A violent group of alt-right, white supremacist supporters of the 45th president hired by billionaires to eliminate threats to their fortunes."

"Okay."

"The surviving 45 was a grand dragon in the KKK. Christine hit him on the face with a drone. One of the Catrinas took him out after that. He had us pinned down."

"Christine didn't mention the bit about the drone."

"You understand how delicate this information is?"

Michelle nodded, miming zipping her lips.

Ella approached followed by black haired Mateis. "Can Mateis and Natalie come to the toy store with us?"

Lane shrugged. "Fine with me. Okay with you Michelle?"

"Okay."

Twenty minutes later they walked along Kensington Road in a loose formation with kids leading the way, adults rushing to catch up while insisting the children wait for them at every corner.

They found Harry Phoenix Toys between coffee shops. The red and white trim around the windows was accented with clear coated maple. The windows showcased life-sized stuffed animals, self-propelled metal cars and handmade scale models of biplanes and locomotives.

Ella and Natalie led the way up the stairs, holding the door open for siblings and elders before pounding up the stairs past them, disappearing behind shelves and display cases.

Michelle said, "Okay you guys, either you slow down or we're outta here."

Lane looked left at the clerk wearing jeans, a white T-shirt and knee-high Mr. Darcy boots. He smiled. She nodded, black hair falling, leaning forward, texting.

He went left as Michelle went right, tracking down kids in between the rows of games, stuffed animals, large and small toys and low flying dragons.

They found all four shoulder to shoulder at the two-metre-long firing range at the back of the store. Foam bullets fired from orange, purple and yellow battery powered toys with zombie eliminator written in lightning on the stocks. Zombies lurched across the back of the neon lit range as luminescent bullets arched before knocking them down.

Lane watched as an elflike zombie flopped after being hit. It let out a long, baritone fart. A much larger zombie in yoga tights was hit, releasing an alto squeaker. Kids' laughter rolled out after each hit.

Ella said, "My turn!"

Lane closed his eyes, savouring the music of their voices.

The tightness in Lauren's chest became more intense as the Tacoma dropped down the long decline into the Qu'Appelle Valley. There were some new buildings along either side of the highway with older structures she recognized from childhood summers. She slowed, coasting through Fort Qu'Appelle, over the river and along the edge of the lake.

Sylvia said, "I need both of you to help decorate the hall after the rehearsal."

Ian looked at Lauren who raised one eyebrow. "Okay."

Sylvia looked out over the lake. "We had some fun times here when you kids were little."

Ian said, "You mean like when we all got duck lice, started to scream from the itching and ended up with all those spots, our bodies dipped in calamine?"

Lauren chuckled. "We were screaming so loud some lady thought you were abusing us. She threatened to call the RCMP."

Sylvia leaned forward, head and shoulders tucked between the front seats.

"I was thinking more about having fun at the beach, sitting around the campfire, watching fireworks."

"That too!" Ian clapped his hands together.

Lauren accelerated up the hill.

Sylvia said, "You know my Katie is pregnant."

A five second silence. Furtive glances between Ian and Lauren waiting to see what Sylvia would say next.

"Two months." Sylvia started to laugh, slapping her son and daughter on their shoulders. "I'm gonna be a grandma!"

Lane sweated up the incline, leaving the river valley, carrying scooters on one shoulder, backpacks on the other. Twenty meters ahead, Indy and Ella pedaled new bikes uphill. As always, Ella was the first to master her bike and its gears. Her older brother caught on out of necessity rather than initiative.

They dropped the bikes on the front lawn, running to the door. Indy opened it first.

"Mom! Uncle Lane bought us new bikes!"

Ella crumpled to sit cross-legged on the step. "I was going to tell her."

Christine came outside, sitting next to Ella, looking at the white and purple bikes. She studied her uncle. She rubbed Ella's back. "Can you show me?"

Ella stood, running, skipping the last few steps, getting on her bike, performing tight turns on the driveway. "It has nine gears." She stopped, looking up at her mom. "I picked out my own." She looked over at Lane. "We wanted to buy zombie guns but he said bikes would be better."

Alexandra came out the front door, preceded by Indy.

Lane smiled. "Buying bikes is the most fun I've had in a long time. Who'd have thought?"

Alexandra put her hand on her sister's shoulder. "Yes, who'd have thought?"

Lane looked at the smiles passing between the sisters. "What?"

Christine said, "Welcome back."

Alexandra stopped, back straightening, head turning. "Karen's awake." She opened the door, going inside.

Indy looked at his mom. "Did you hear Karen?"

Christine tapped an earlobe. "Mom's newborn ears."

Indy shook his head.

Christine looked at her uncle. "What do you want for supper?"

Lauren stopped at a gas station on the north side of Kenton. Ian stepped out, stretching his legs. Sylvia sat on the tailgate, puffing out clouds of vaped apple. A green jacked up pickup started up, its diesel motor wheezing then roaring as the driver stood on the brakes, tailpipe shitting a cloud of black smoke.

Ian looked at his sister, seeing that she recognized the driver. The last time she'd seen Steve, he'd had his left arm in a cast. Now his arm was on the wheel. He wore a green Saskatchewan Rough Riders' ball cap. His double chin quivered from the truck's vibration.

Ian asked, "Want to break his other arm?"

Sylvia puffed another vape cloud. With her free hand, she

waved at Steve. His response was to release the brakes. The rear wheels shuddered He swerved out onto Main Street, leaving behind the black air to drift east down the alley.

"He played one game in the NHL." Ian said, "Scored on his own goalie."

Lauren exhaled slowly. *It's Kate's wedding. Don't start anything.*

YYC NEWS LIVE

(INT - Studio news set - Anchor Stephanie Ozduran sits next to Natasha Summerville at news desk.)

"I'm Stephanie Ozduran and this is YYC News Live. Natasha Summerville joins me in studio for an update on what is being called the Catrina Revolution. Natasha, can you share more details with us on the extraordinary events and the local connection to this story?"

"Well, Stephanie, people appear to have two opinions about the Catrinas. The people who lost money are calling them thieves. A series of recent polls shows between eighty-five and ninety per cent of the population see the Catrinas as heroines. And it appears that Canadian, Mexican and American authorities are siding with the majority as a series of warrants have been issued. Murder and attempted murder charges were laid against Moby and Curtis Drayten. The pair of billionaires are reported to be in the Cayman Islands. Since the Caymans have no extradition treaties, the pair may be able to avoid arrest. The U.S. and Canadian governments have already frozen all Drayten assets."

"The local connection to this story has some fascinating angles. There are consistent reports that at least two and perhaps as many as four Catrinas are from Calgary. We are working hard to confirm these reports. One individual has been contacted and has agreed to an interview with YYC

NEWS next week."

"Thanks for the update, Natasha. Make sure to join us on YYC News Monday for the interview with an anonymous source connected to the Catrinas story. Thanks for watching YYC News."

Lauren inhaled her sister's scent. It was a blend of soft soap, gentle perfume and homemade sausage.

They were outside on Sylvia's deck. The evening sun shone through the barbecue smoke.

Kate whispered in her sister's ear. "I'm pregnant. Two months." She was a bit shorter than Lauren with dirty blonde hair, blue eyes, an almond shaped face and bright white smile.

Lauren inhaled, catching a strand of Kate's hair in her mouth, spitting, whispering, "Mom told us on the way in. She's pretty excited."

Kate pushed her sister back, seeing her pulling hair from her mouth, smiling. "Oops."

"Do Riley's parents know?"

Riley, Kate's fiancé, sat drinking a cold one on the deck with Ian, who detested beer but was doing his best to be hospitable.

Riley was a graphic novel illustrator who lived in Saskatoon among its burgeoning artistic community. Kate had started up a medical practice after doing her internship there. Riley was round, had a red beard, short brown hair, brown eyes and a ready smile.

Lauren asked, "Okay if I get Ian a glass of wine before he leans over the deck and barfs into the bushes?"

Kate hugged her tighter. "I appreciate you making the trip. Will you come and see us in Saskatoon? I'd like it if you there when the baby comes."

Lauren began to sob. *Shit! Now it happens!*

Ian stood, setting his beer on the railing. "Lauren? You

okay?"

They sat her in Ian's chair as Sylvia came outside with a tray of buns, condiments and potato salad.

Kate asked, "What's happening?"

Ian said, "Lauren had to kill a guy last week in Mexico. I've been expecting this. Hashir asked me to keep an eye out. You know how she is. Holding it together, then it hits her."

Sylvia asked, "Who's Hashir?"

"A guy she works with. He phoned to tell me about it. Lauren has time off because of it. She's supposed to see a shrink when we get back."

Sylvia set the tray down before wrapping her arms around Lauren. "What did those bastards do to my girl?"

CHAPTER 16

Lauren wore a navy blue and white striped summer dress, standing alongside Kate, Ian and Riley.

Father Macpherson officiated the service. He was a local boy who'd gone away, returning as a priest to the surprise of almost everyone in the congregation. He stood over six feet with a bit of a spare tire protruding from under his white cassock. His head shone under the light streaming through the stained-glass windows. Macpherson's once red hair had fallen out along with most of his wild child rebellious streak. Now he looked over the heads of the wedding party, making deliberate eye contact with the congregation.

Lauren tensed, remembering the rote phrase from past weddings. She looked right at Ian with his neon green hair, tailored silver suit and neon green running shoes. Lauren inhaled, expecting to hear, "Marriage is a sacrament between a man and a woman." The moment in the ceremony she'd been dreading, knowing in her present state of mind she would respond, defending her brother, embarrassing her sister, causing another stir in Kenton, reminding everyone of her past offences.

She inhaled along with Father Macpherson before he said, "Marriage is a sacrament between..." He hesitated.

Lauren glanced at her brother, opening her mouth.

"... people who love one another. This wedding is a celebration of love, commitment and family."

Lauren looked at Macpherson, catching the briefest of winks – the whisper of a smile. She inhaled, feeling her sister's hand in hers, seeing her grin through tears.

CHAPTER 17

Anna sat beside Lauren at Xtravagant Hair. Lori's hair stylist had agreed to open her salon for them. She'd arranged for six face painters and makeup artists willing to prepare the group for the YYC News interview. "How was the wedding?"

Lauren said, "It was good. I'm gonna be an auntie."

Anna asked, "When?"

"Early December. Kate wants me to be there with her in Saskatoon. I'm excited." She looked in the mirror, not recognizing herself with the base layer of black, the white scar running from her left eye along a lazy arc to her chin. There were white skeletal circles around her eye sockets. The artists found themselves constantly reassuring the six Catrinas none would be recognizable after the makeup was done.

Rhonda tried on a cowboy hat someone must have sat on. "Being an aunt is the best."

Lane nodded, checking his red skeletal smile in the mirror. "My niece and nephew are awesome."

Lori lifted her red beret. "Being a grandma is pretty awesome. Don't forget the bus'll be here soon."

Christine asked, "Why a school bus?"

Rhonda said, "Nobody pays any attention to a yellow bus."

Lori checked her beret's angle in the mirror. "When you

hear two beeps from my phone, that'll mean our ride is ready and it'll be time for us to end the interview."

YYC NEWS LIVE

(INT - YYC News Anchor and reporter sit opposite a group of six people whose faces are disguised with facepaint.)

"Hello, I'm Stephanie Ozduran, for YYC News Live. Natasha Summerville and I are at an undisclosed location in Calgary. We are delighted to have six Catrinas in attendance, local members of the group who some are calling heroes while others decry them as criminals. Catrinas, how do you respond to being labelled criminals?"

Lori wore a blue beret and a red and black quilted skeletal face. She spoke while the other Catrinas sat in shadow. Lori's voice was disguised. "Criminals plan to profit from their crimes. Not one Catrina has profited from the recovery of moneys illegally stashed in tax havens."

Natasha asked, "There are six of you–five women and one man. Are you representative of the larger group?"

Anna wore a black top hat and keyboard painted across her skeletal forehead. "The majority of us are female."

Stephanie said, "Last week there was a gun battle on Stoney Trail. Was it connected to the Catrinas and the secretive group known as the 45s?"

Lauren wore a pink sun hat. Her white eye sockets were more pronounced than the others. "Yes."

"In what way?"

Lauren said, "I can only answer your question in very general terms. The police are conducting interviews of the various suspects involved. Evidence is being gathered. It's important to note that warrants for arrests have been issued for individuals presently outside of North America. The 45s are a violent terrorist group."

Stephanie leaned forward, lifting her chin at Lauren. "You know this how?"

"I was there when four heavily armed U.S. citizens – one of whom Mexican and US officials confirmed was a Grand Dragon in the KKK – attacked with the intent of murdering all of us. We fought them off and captured two who are in the custody of Mexican authorities."

Stephanie asked, "And the other two? You said there were four."

"Dead."

Christine wore a bowler hat and a white handlebar moustache. "She saved my life."

Lane lifted his pith helmet. His face wore a broad white and red skeletal smile. "And mine."

Stephanie pointed at them. "You witnessed this?"

Lane nodded. "The grand dragon was shooting at us. She stopped him." He pointed at Scar Face.

Anna lifted a manila folder. "In here you will find documents detailing the specific amounts taken from illegal offshore accounts. The itemized documents have converted all currencies from the various accounts into US dollars. Every penny is accounted for. As you already know more than $2 trillion have been set aside to provide clean water in North America. The remaining $15 trillion will be used to support various initiatives aimed at improving the lives of lower income individuals in North America. And that..." she stood as Lori's phone beeped twice. "That is all we have to say for the moment. If you require further information," she pointed at Natasha, "You know how to contact us."

"One more question." Stephanie stood. "Why the Catrina makeup? What are you hiding?"

Lauren laughed. "There have been attempts in Mexico, Calgary and Edmonton to eliminate us. I should think the answer is obvious."

She followed Anna out the door with the rest of the Catrinas behind. They walked to the back door of the empty shop. Anna opened the door to be greeted by cameras, microphones and reporters.

Lori said, "Own it."

They stepped into the sun, backs to the grey wall, facing a four storey condo complex.

One reporter spoke above the rest. "Reuben Denver CEO Mustang Media." He had salt and pepper hair, a round face and pastrami lips. He wore his trademark blue blazer.

Lori saw Anna pull out her phone, her fingers dancing across the screen.

Reuben said, "You are common criminals masquerading as lefty do-gooders. It's only a matter of time before you are arrested."

Lori smiled. "Seventeen trillion dollars was stolen from ordinary North American citizens. That money has been recovered."

Reuben said, "No one believes you haven't profited from the theft."

Anna held up her phone. "Mr. Denver you have $13.7 million hidden in offshore accounts. You are hardly in a position to judge."

Reuben exploded. "My finances are not in question here! You are nothing but a backyard hacker!"

Laughter rippled behind Denver who said, "It's a lie!"

Another reporter ignored Reuben, moving his microphone near Lauren. "What can you tell us about the 45s?"

Lauren said, "Take a look at the FresaLeaks website. It has accurate information about the group, its members, affiliations and the money behind them."

A second reporter asked, "What is your motivation?"

Lane said, "It was a job that needed doing."

Lauren saw a yellow school bus driving up the alley between the reporters and the construction area. "A sexual predator was elected president. That was the final straw as far as many of us are concerned."

"Our ride is here. Any other questions?" Lori began an end

run around the reporters, heading for the bus. The Catrinas followed.

As she passed a third reporter, he asked, "Why the makeup?"

Lauren asked, "You ever been shot at?"

The reporter shook his head. "Not yet."

Lauren followed Lane onto the bus. She stepped up, turning to face the crowd. "When you've been shot at, then you can ask that question." She turned around, the doors of the bus closing behind her.

Cameras focused on the side of the bus. Five Catrinas were framed in the windows as the bus bumped along the alley, heading west.

Christine said, "They're getting in their cars to follow us."

Lori laughed. "No worries. My boys have got this." She pointed at a dumpster. Two men pushed it, blocking the lane as the bus passed. Lori's sons escaped down a narrow passageway between buildings.

Rhonda took off her battered cowboy hat. "Glad that's over."

Lauren shook her head, removing her pink sun hat, tossing it on the seat across. "Over? This thing is just getting started."

Acknowledgments

Thank you Doctor Navaid. And thank you to the caregivers at Sarcee Hospice.

Thanks to the late Wayne Gunn.

Thank you, Leslie Vermeer for being a long-time editor of the Detective Lane books. You are a gifted teacher. This novel has your fringerprints all over it. All the smudges are mine.

Thank you, Richard Young for the invaluable coffee shop advice, insights, and openness to this venture. Kendra and Jeremy, thank you for making the book so much better.

Thanks to Pages, The Next Page, Owl's Nest, Shelf Life, and all independent booksellers who support local writers.

Thanks to web designer Stephen.

Thanks to creative writers at Nickle, Bowness, Lord Beaverbrook, Alternative, Forest Lawn, and Queen Elizabeth.

Sharon, Karma, Ben, Luke, Indiana, Ella, and Parisa.

This is for you

Garry Ryan

Winner of the *Lambda Literary Prize* and recipient of Calgary's *Freedom of Expression Award*, author Garry Ryan drinks mochas and lives in Calgary, Alberta.

www.garryryan.ca